Nights of Blue

Jacqueline Fernandez

~

Dedicated to my loving parents and family
who have encouraged me to follow my dreams.

~

I would like to thank God in Heaven above.

I am grateful to Lisa, Tanes, Lou, Sulema and Erika for reading my manuscript and giving me invaluable forthright comments and suggestions.

To the muse who is my vehicle of creative inspiration.

I would like to acknowledge the support and encouragement I have received from my parents Maria and Heriberto Fernandez; my siblings Ruth, Sulema, Jesus, and Heriberto Jr.

Special thanks to Mr. Putthiporn and Mr. Beckert for motivating me to write and tell my stories.

1

The sun's rays penetrate the earth like a whip scorching a body mercilessly. Guanajuato - *a picturesque place full of virgin landscape, embraced by rock formations locking the magic within.* It is a natural beauty that allows for the inconvenience of the humidity and heat. The journey, is sweetly enhanced by the aromatic scent of gardenias and foliage, serve to seductively draw you in. Indeed, Guanajuato is a colloquial place of grace and charm. The Spanish were clever in wanting to leave their mark on such a place, establishing cobblestone roads. It is forever young resenting growing old. It is a timeless world that stands still with the passage of years, holding on to the breast of nature in order to continue suckling the dew of youth. It seems earth has surrendered her love to this child that has seized to further grow.

The sudden halt of the horses made a quick stop in front of a lovely hacienda. It is the Hacienda of San Gabriel that holds much mystery behind the ornate iron walls, handcrafted with perfection, laced with white flowers to accentuate its surrounding. As you approach the gates it's protected by two stones lions much like the Canova lions that form part of the Rezzonico Monument in St Peter's Rome.

Clarissa and her Aunt step out of the carriage to closely observe this place of interest. Clarissa stands transfixed on the beauty of the sculptured lion's face. She is overcome by strange emotions. Her aunt, unaware, walks ahead realizing a few seconds later that her niece has stopped behind. Tia Maria, as she was called, had very little patience especially when the weather proved unbearable. Her niece was different from most girls. She was fortunate, receiving a proper education abroad and enjoying a cultured taste of life. Clarissa was a silly romantic, Tia Maria was practical, and the ideas of romantic love were an absurd notion. The most a girl could hope for would be for a man to be a good provider and father. Tia Maria felt Clarissa foolish with strange ideas of perfect love that simply does not exist. It could only bring disappointment and sorrow. Too much sun was now irritating Tia Maria.

"Clarissa, come along child! You wanted to come here and here we are young lady. We have little time to trespass on the owner's property. It is best to give them their privacy."

Clarissa had come to Guanajuato as a small child and was impressed by the vastness of trees that canopied the entrance and the sweet sound of the wind, rumbling through the leaves. She begged her parents to take her back again the desire of this place haunted her in her dreams. She was excited to have her dream come true after so many years.

"Tia, I am so happy! I cannot believe that I am really here." Clarissa's voice was filled with joy. "I have been anxious to see all this again. I have always imagined myself belonging to this place." Tia Maria smiled at her niece amusingly. Her innocence made her look so angelic.

"Clarissa you are such an imaginative and romantic child." They walked together through the great estate leaving the lions behind. "Clarissa, do you want to go to the chapel or explore the gardens of Don Andres?"

"What can you tell me about Don Andres, Tia?" Tia Maria stood pensive and nodded her head as if conversing to herself. "It is indeed lamentable. He is a man of great wealth that carries a burden. He is said to have suffered greatly, he has wept a valley of tears from a wounded heart. His consolation is that he has a devoted son that frequents him."

"Tia, is he a widower?" Tia Maria dryly disagrees. "His wife left him many years ago. It was said she was bitter and resented him, tired of living the lie of a perfect family. She cursed him every day of unhappiness he gave her. It is said his heart belonged to another. I do not quite remember the details. Nonetheless, it was a private matter that few speak of and therefore left for fantastic speculations."

The Hacienda had the gardens of the world represented; each had its own mystique from cactus flower to the velvety rose and the majestic trees of Europe. In a secluded part of the garden, a mosaic blue fountain made Clarissa's chest heave, engrossed in a dream like state, she recites to herself in a low voice, "This place is alien yet so familiar. My heart aches for this man's broken spirit." She contemplated Don Andres as she observed ivy walls with colorful roses. It was easy to lose one self in the tranquility of the garden, taking in the melodic sound of the fountain orchestrating rhythm as well as the fragrance of the garden.

"How Eve must have felt leaving Paradise as there is not enough breath in the air to absorb this place. I think of all I have read and remember the poet Wordworth, these beauteous forms." Clarissa looks to the sky as she stretches her arms to the heavens. She looks away from the sky above and sighs deeply. "I feel ecstasy in this moment that I could happily die and not resent what the rest of my life may be. This garden of paradise, glorious alters of trees arch to make pathways of promise upon green velvet carpet." She walks to a set of rose bushes that captivate her with their texture. She caresses its petals. "My imagination, sparked with the wondrous dreams as the smells of the fragrance flowers, sweet and subtle ease my spirit."

She speaks to the flower in her hands. "Oh Eve, how could you have eaten the fruit of deceit, to cast you and your lover from such paradise. To be exiled to nothingness by vanity." She walks to the fountain and gently drops a few droplets of water to the freshly cut flower. The spirit of the poet within emerges. "A poetic rebirth grows in my womb cast by the intoxication of this place, from these sweet flowers to the exotic and rustic cactuses that stir anxiousness within."

The agony of the man who resides here envelopes her. His home is so full of pain. The tears begin to roll slowly down her cheeks as she looks at the reflection of her face in the fountain. Clarissa feels an intense empathy and is uncomfortable with the emergence of the strange emotions inside her. "What is wrong with me? I do not understand what is happening to me. I look at this watery mirror and reflected is an unspeakable sorrow behind my eyes. Years of repressed anguish; I must

6

leave this place. The heat and excitement has me imaging such silly ideas." She turns away and goes to the chapel in hopes for some rationality and consolation to these awkward feelings.

The chapel is a vision of reverence and exuberant beauty. It is bathed in gold and silk. The alter is ornate with its filigree podium and white flowers that sit on each side in gilded vases with the portrait of the Virgin of Guadalupe in the center, decorated with gold leaf around her. A haven in style and grace, accentuated by the white flowers that shower the chapel. The aisles are illuminated with the flicker of candles. Clarissa rushes in but realizing the sacredness of the place, she slows her pace. Her aunt is close, lighting a candle for a special blessing on her household. After lighting the candle, she waits for her niece to finish her prayers. Clarissa stands up to the splendor of the chapel in awe.

"Tia, this place is charming yet disturbing." Her aunt responds lightly, "Child, you will quickly learn that all of Guanajuato is under one enchanting spell that lives in the past, present and future. All is one in this place. Now we must depart, for I have to get a few items for supper…mole sounds good today." Clarissa nods and follows her aunt out of the chapel.

All is an eternal dream in Guanajuato, charming and quaint. The carriage stops by the great Theatre that surrounds the artisan shops, food markets, and impressive cathedral. In the center is a garden gazebo crown to adorn it. Melodic echoes filter through the air, narrators singing through the cobblestone streets lyrically retelling the stories that embrace Guanajuato. Tia Maria rushes to the poultry shop to get fresh chicken for tonight's meal. Clarissa follows distractedly and decides to head toward the gazebo rather than stay in the carriage. She excuses herself and promises to stay close while her aunt completes her errands.

Clarissa is taken with the gazebo made up of a lovely skirt of small flowers with trees arching above it. Its benches are situated for secluded romantic inducement and declarations of secret sentiments. By day, the sky is serenity of blue tranquility and by night a kaleidoscope of brilliant stars and a brilliant moon. Affected Clarissa closes her eyes and speaks from her heart. "How blessed to be among such tranquility." A tingling sensation runs through her body, similar to her experience at the Hacienda. Her eyes open to a man walking up the steps of the Cathedral.

Her eyes focus on the image. She is compelled to follow him. She follows a few steps behind. At the Cathedral Clarissa realizes her yearning to glimpse into this man's eyes. Clarissa walks in; there he is before the cross. It is dark and solemn inside the cathedral. Religious images hide on the walls, like shadows hidden by the clouds. The only hope lies in the few lit candles. His melancholy lingers around him. Clarissa feels the warmth of his body and his sadness, which reins his heart.

Don Luis Andres is a robust man of grand stature. He is dressed impeccably and handsome in his old age. Pain swims in his eyes, his lips are absent of happiness. He holds a candle in the Cathedral to light a prayer for the mystery in his life. A sudden breeze blows in and dims the Cathedral, veiling it in darkness. Clarissa is paralyzed with fear and looks around for a glimpse of light in the confusion of her mind. The light from Heaven slowly begins to illuminate the Cathedral. He stands before her staring in disbelief. His eyes ... his face ... all too familiar. Clarissa utters unconsciously, "I know him!"

He walks with a glow of sweet ecstasy as if approaching an apparition. Clarissa cannot help but stare in return. Despite his age, she finds him so handsome. Never has she seen such a lovely man. His tears are apparent as he walks toward her. Clarissa is unable to run away. Anxiety and delight are tearing within her. Her eyes begin to grow as he speaks softly. "My only love, Clarissa, don't you know me?" His tears continue to flow as he speaks to the vision of his love he has guarded so long in his heart.

Clarissa's heart feels united with this man despite her mind trying to make sense of it. She is captivated by his presence near her. Her thoughts are for him only. "His eyes are calm and unsettling like the green waters." She closes her eyes to these strange thoughts. He caresses her face ever so gentle, trembling with fear that she might not exist. Clarissa opens her eyes and looks beyond the color of his eyes to see him as he was many years ago. The tears pour from Clarissa. She remembers him as the mysteries unlock from the back of her unconsciousness, in a light breath, "Luis Andres!" He embraces her and holds her tightly afraid to lose her again.

"You have come back to me Clarissa. I never stopped loving you." Weeping with unleashed agony, "I am so sorry; please forgive me for making us so unhappy." He releases her for a moment only to take something from his pocket. "Clarissa, do you remember this? I gave it to you many years ago."

It was a lovely necklace with small precious stones. His voice was tired but unusually excited. The necklace shimmered and reflected its brilliancy of colors with the light of the candles. Don Luis Andres placed the necklace around Clarissa's neck sweetly and kissed her. Clarissa, never touched by a man, yet his caresses seemed familiar. He takes hold of her hand and places it on his chest. "Feel how happy you have made me, my love."

She looks into his eyes and they lock. Their breath draws closer and closer until she feels his lips on hers. She tastes his soul becoming one breath. Both feel the warm tears dripping down their faces. A whirlwind of emotions and thoughts swirl in Clarissa's head. A fog of darkness descends with no warning. A sudden slumber of oblivion hits her. The song of quiet words echo in her ears as she meets the floor with tenderness. "Te amo, my love until eternity."

Caressingly, Don Luis Andres takes his coat and places it under her head as she lay still. He touches her soft hair. It is difficult for him to comprehend that she lay young and beautiful with lips so sweet. He realizes that she belongs to the present time. He kneels and touches the necklace around her neck. His hand moves toward her face as he bends down to kiss the lips that he had kissed so long ago and still burn in his memory. It is time to leave. The agony of having to part from her is unbearable and feels like dying again. He walks slowly away dreaming of the day they would be reunited again. Don Luis Andres walks to the Hacienda, aware of the differences in their ages. He sighs great knowing his youth is gone. His life has made a complete circle.

2

The scent of frankincense is faint but overpowering. Clarissa's mind begins to clear and regain awareness. She wakes from a heavy dream to the confusion of being watched by a priest and his flock of small children. "Are you alright child?" asks the priest in a surprised tone.

"What happened to me? I was outside enjoying the day and saw a man and … It must have been just a silly dream." Suddenly aware of her rambling she stands up with his help. "Oh Father forgive me."

The priest looks at her with familiarity. "You were lying on the floor. I was afraid …"

She interrupts him as she notices the coat used to elevate her head for comfort. She speaks to herself minding those around her. "He left his coat … then it must have happened, but it cannot be!"

The priest recognizes the coat and confirms his suspicion but it is impossible. He stares profoundly in disbelief. Clarissa is aware that the priest is looking at her with interest. She cannot help but feel that he too is familiar somehow. She speaks sweetly, "Father, thank you for your kindness. I am sorry to have caused so much trouble. It must have been the long journey that exhausted me." She hesitated before asking about Don Luis Andres. "Did you happen to see an older gentleman?"

Knowing whom she refers to, the priest says somberly "No my child, I did not see anyone leave the Cathedral."

She gives him her hand and he holds it for a moment observing the softness of it. Clarissa is uneasy again trying to shake these feelings that were mounting inside her. As if remembering her manners, she introduces herself formerly to the priest. "Father, I am Clarissa de la Luz." The priest is stunned by the enunciation of her first name. His voice is nervous as he slowly repeats her name. She looks perplexed while the children around say nothing. The weariness is taking a toll on her spirit. She feels worn by the strange occurrences. There is something in the Priest that nudges her memory. "Father have we met before? I know you from somewhere. As a child maybe?" The pupil of his eyes light in amazement

Tia Maria is nervous that Clarissa was nowhere to be found. She goes through all the shops that could spark her interest. It occurs to her to walk to the Cathedral. She sees her niece surrounded by the priest and a flock of small children. She is not happy as she walks briskly with authority in her steps. "Father, I am sorry if my niece was any trouble. She is easily distracted." She gives her a stern look that makes Clarissa lower her head. The priest notices the aunt's expression and places his hand on her shoulders to ease her frustration.

Tia Maria is of a generous temperament but easily annoyed since she has no children. She loves Clarissa greatly despite the views of her education. To Tia Maria, Clarissa has been hindered by the liberal education she has received. "Dona Maria there is no need to be upset with this charming girl. It is obvious that she is tired from such a long journey." Her aunt quickly forgets her anger and conveys a voice of concern. "Clarissa I must get you home to rest before dinner. Father Roberto, thank you. It has been a long time since this child was here and is not used to the heat."

He nods his head in agreement. He releases a deep sigh and looks at Clarissa who still hangs her head in embarrassment. His eyes take notice of a familiar item of long ago. Clarissa aware that Father Roberto has noticed the necklace shyly places it under her collar. He moves forward and extends his hand. "Clarissa it is indeed a pleasure seeing you. "Please come and visit me when you are settled. I am sure we have much to talk about." She smiles as she nods her head in agreement.

In the carriage Tia Maria holds her niece's hand with concern over her physical disposition. "Ay Clarissa you gave me a scare. What am I going to do with you? It looked like Father Roberto was picking you up from the floor. Did you fall? He was so pale at your sight, something must have happened."

Clarissa places her hand over her aunt's in hope to ease her mind. She attempts to explain. "Tia, I apologize for making you worry. It was just that …" Her aunt looks at her disconcerted that Clarissa decides it is best not to say what truly happened. How could she even begin to explain when she did not understand herself? "It was too much sun exposure." The warm reminder around her neck is the evidence that something is changing in her life.

Father Roberto is reminded of the past. He walks through the corridors of the Cathedral. The haunting image of the young girl brings painful memories of his youth. He walks slowly into his room and heads toward the window. He turns the latch and opens the window. Father Roberto closes his eyes and takes in all the fresh air his lungs can hold. His body is tired. The emotions he thought were buried came crawling back. The image of her face is burned in his mind with the bold vividness of her eyes. So many years later. A cruel reminder of the past incarnated in a youthful body. He loved her still even after all these years. A small tear falls from the corner of his eye. His thoughts are many. It is as if Clarissa stayed still in time while everyone around her grew old. He is struck with the realization that Clarissa met Don Luis Andres. He fears that the reunion may unravel a tragedy. He will visit Don Luis Andres and discover exactly what took place in his church.

Tia Maria's house is lovely with simple warmth and beauty. The house is yellow with green borders and an inviting veranda with flowerpots to give it atmosphere. As they approach the house Clarissa is engrossed with thoughts of the gentleman who had given the gift around her neck. It slips her mind that she is at the place she yearned to visit again. Her aunt warned her that this place is enchanted. The horses come to a halt; the help come out to welcome them. Tia Maria worries her niece is coming down with something.

"You look pale my child. I want you to go to your room and rest while I prepare you some chamomile tea and supper."

Clarissa kisses her aunt on the cheek, "Tia you are too sweet and kind to me. It is no wonder I love you so much."

Tia Maria lightly laughs. "As much as your mother?"

Clarissa gives her another kiss. "Do not tell her but just the same."

Tia Maria nods her head. "Go rest. I will have one of the girls bring your tea."

Clarissa does not want her aunt to fuss over her. "No Tia, after a nice bath and sleep I will be like new."

They walk into the house and her aunt calls for one of the girls. "Mella! Take my niece to her room and draw her bath." The girl curtsies in obedience and smiles at Clarissa.

Mella is a spirited delightful girl. She is indigenous with golden olive skin that glistens. It is difficult still for some to find respect for one that is indigenous despite their pedigree heritage. They are the children of the Mighty Sun King that once ruled this rich land and Mella belongs to that legacy. "Niña Clarissa, follow me to your room." She directs her upstairs. Mella continues to talk of how excited they are to have her there. Clarissa listens to her and smiles as her mind travels into oblivion to the incidents that transpired in the Cathedral and the familiarity of Father Roberto.

Mella opens the door to Clarissa's room. It is serene, detailed with painted flowers over the borders of the walls. The windows are open to let the breeze blow in. A vase sits close to the windowsill with freshly cut gardenias. Her favorite books wait for her on the desk. A small door opens to the balcony outside. Clarissa studies her view. The sun is beginning to set and the Cathedral can be seen from her balcony. It is a beautiful panoramic scene. Mella's voice interrupts her thoughts. "Niña Clarissa you look faint. What may I bring you?"

Clarissa turns and embraces Mella. "I am not myself today but thank you for your concern."

Mella is surprised by the sudden sign of affection. "Niña Clarissa do you want me to prepare your bath?"

Clarissa releases a smile. "No, thank you very much. I can draw my own bath."

Mella, happy that Doña Maria's niece is amiable responds, "I am glad you are here especially for Doña Maria who loves you very much."

Clarissa smiles thoughtfully. "Yes I know. I am blessed. She is a wonderful lady." Clarissa moves toward the door of her balcony and looks out. "Mella, just bring me tea.' She exits the door leaving Clarissa alone.

Clarissa looks out to the view of her window and begins to caress her lips reminded of the warmth of his breath again in her head. The landscape before her is transforming into darkness. She feels a cold light wind penetrate her bones. She wonders about what the future has in store for her. She reveals the secret beneath her collar. She admires the intricacy of its beauty. It is peculiar that his necklace is recognizable to her. She removes it from her neck and places it on the bureau. She feels anxiety at the thought of parting from it. She takes the necklace into the bathroom where she begins to prepare her bath. Clarissa lets the steam from the hot water fill the room. She begins to undress when she hears her aunt come in.

"Clarissa are you alright my child?" Tia Maria knocks on the bathroom door. Clarissa quickly buries the necklace under some towels. She knows that speculation on how she obtained it could create problems for her.

14

Instead she moves to the door and peaks out to greet her. "Tia I am just about to take a bath. I am very fatigued from the trip that I am going to turn in early."

Tia Maria is disappointed but understands. "I brought you a tea and sweet roll." She paused for a moment before continuing. "Clarissa if you decide to join us I prepared your favorite mole for dinner. Nevertheless I will have them save you some for later."

Clarissa gratefully blows a kiss to her in appreciation. "Thank you Tia for everything." Doña Maria closes the door behind her. Clarissa waits until she hears her completely depart and with her robe around her body walks to lock the door of her room to ensure privacy.

Clarissa heads to the bathroom and uncovers the treasure hidden among the towels. Clarissa proceeds to light the candles to brighten the room and slips into the hot water that is waiting for her. She is not afraid to allow the miracle to take place in her mind. It is like a dream. The necklace in her hand is more captivating in the water. She recalls those eyes that yearn to know her. She envisions a sweet fantasy where they dance in the night surrounded by the freshness of the air with cool passions as they move slowly under the stars. Clarissa looks into those eyes that had her heart imprinted on them. The soft echoes of nature's music can be heard as they continue to dance to the movement of their love. Her breath stands still to see him as she knew long ago. It is then the water from her bath goes up her nose to rudely wake her.

"What is happening to me?" She stands up abruptly and notices all the candles are extinguished except the ones she had lit. Clarissa places the necklace on her neck and dries herself and dresses in her sleeping gown. It is difficult to ascertain what is transpiring inside her. She paces up and down her room and takes a sip of her cold tea. She goes to the window and opens it wider. The night welcomes her with its sweet smell.

"Something is happening to me and I do not know what to do?" She looks to the moon in the sky. "Please God help ease this anxiousness that is growing steadily within for this strange man." A soft breeze resonates his name in her ears. Her mind is infiltrated with thoughts of him. Her bed draped in soft whiteness awaits her. Clarissa did not want to think of him any longer. She climbs into the sheets and melts into the coolness of the night. Exhausted by the mysteries around her with a deep sigh she falls into a slumber sleep.

3

The house is made up of two humble rooms. The bedroom has a
wooden bed and the kitchen, which also has a spare bed. The house is
petite and inviting. The portraits of the Virgin Mary and Jesus Christ have
a vigilant candle lit daily. The stove is made of brick with a clay pot above
it for simmering beans. There is a small garden made of flowers, fruits
and vegetables. A table with a bench is outside for those rare moments
with friends to eat. It is pleasant and more than neighboring families had.
The everyday life of the poor is to learn to be hard working, obedient and
thankful for the communion of God and the family, which give daily
insight.

The old man calls to his daughter. "Clarissa! Clarissa! We cannot be late."
The young girl is having her hair braided by her mother. It is unusual for
a girl of poor upbringing to carry a name like Clarissa. It is expected
mostly to have saintly names as to ensure blessings from above. Her
mother is scrutinized for giving her only child a name perceived to be
pretentious. Guadalupe does not identify it that way. She heard the name
from the lips of her Patrona. It sounded so musical, she felt it befitting to
a princess. The seed of her life that almost cost her life. It bothers her
husband Jacinto but he loves his wife and therefore lets it be.

"I am sorry Papa. I will be out in a moment. I must look presentable to La Patrona."

Jacinto adores his child. She is lovely and now a young woman. "Clarissa, do as we tell you. Doña Santos is a delicate woman. The rich are funny people, my child. Remember to only speak when spoken to." Clarissa listens attentively to her father.

Guadalupe comes to bid them farewell. "I will see you later in the big house."

Clarissa and Jacinto wave back in anticipation. They walk toward the big house and the dirt road that leads there. Jacinto continues to talk to his child. "Clarissa you are now of age to help us. We have worked for the Santos family for a long time. It is there I met your lovely mother." Clarissa enjoys how her father gleams at the mention of her mother's name. "It is one of the better wealthy households to work for. Unfortunately there is no justice if a poor offends a rich, keep that in mind. It was only yesterday a man from a neighboring hacienda was almost beaten to death for accidentally killing a priced pig that escaped from the stable."

Clarissa is astounded by her father's tale. "Papa you have never been treated in such a way."

"No, my child. I have yet to give the Patrones a reason."

They walk through the countryside talking. This will be the first time she will step inside the grandiose house. "Clarissa, remember your place in this household. We come here to work only."

She nods and pats her father on his back. "Papa, do not worry. I understand clearly."

A carriage approaches them from behind. It is Roberto who is a young man who owns some property his parents left behind after their untimely death. He is a dear friend and respected in town. He has strong affections for Clarissa. Her family hoped that a union between this young man and Clarissa would take place soon. He is handsome whose hands have seen hard work. They have calluses from working his land and other things. His heart was full every time he bestowed his sight on Clarissa. She has grown up before his eyes into a captivating young woman. He is five years her senior.

"Señor Jacinto, are you going to the big house?"

Clarissa interrupts. "Roberto today is my first day working. We are headed there as we speak."

Roberto enjoys hearing her speak.

"Roberto, would you be so kind to take Clarissa the rest of the way? This would help me as I have another errand to run for the Patrones."

Clarissa is surprised. However, Roberto is ecstatic and quickly accepts the request. "Señor Jacinto, it is no problem. I will gladly take Clarissa to her first day at work". She is content to know that she will not have to walk the rest of the way. They both wave to Jacinto as they head to the Hacienda.

As they arrive to the Hacienda it is not difficult to see the grounds are the best around. The house is unspeakably glorious and green. Roberto stops the carriage a few feet from the house and looks at Clarissa with some concern. His eyes are filled with silent emotion. "Clarissa, promise me you will be careful. Do not let anyone speak to you alone, especially the men of the household. Also, try not to bring attention to yourself."

Clarissa is startled by this sudden concern. She cares greatly for him. He is an important person in her life and assumes that in time she will marry him. "Roberto, do not be afraid for me. You forget that my parents work close to me."

He looks at her attentively. She is indeed a young woman with her own strong character wrapped in sweetness. He will not allow his insecurities to ruin his time with her.

They proceed to the back of the house. The house is in preparation for the arrival of guests, specifically the son of the Patrones. Consuelo comes to greet them. She is a robust yet charming woman. She moves forward and embraces Clarissa heartedly. "You are indeed a lovely creature. I cannot say I am surprised, your parents are handsome enough." She looks at Roberto and smiles amusingly. "Is this handsome young man your boyfriend?" Clarissa and Roberto are taken by surprise by her bold insinuation. "It is obvious that he is taken by you."

Clarissa cannot look at Roberto without embarrassment. She quietly notes that they are old friends.

Consuelo nods her head suspiciously. "Well I am obligated to get you ready to meet Doña Santos." Clarissa feels the nerves reach her stomach, unleashing butterflies. She turns to bid Roberto farewell and gives him a kiss on the cheek. He holds her hand quickly and asks if she wants to be picked up. Consuelo enjoys the scenery before her. She interrupts the interlude. "Clarissa will be staying the night but you can pick her up tomorrow after the festivities are over." Roberto excuses himself from the women and parts bashfully, promising to return tomorrow to pick up Clarissa. Consuelo gives a laugh. "An old friend? Well I think there may be something else in store behind those eyes of his."

Clarissa felt it best to say nothing but smile.

There is much excitement around the kitchen with all the preparation of food for the anticipated event. Clarissa follows Consuelo through the house. It is breathtaking to see all the beautiful things displayed. The Grecian vases with flowers and sculptors placed throughout the house. They approach the large mahogany doors to enter the bureau. It is intimidating to see the stature of the doors that are protecting whatever lies inside from the world outside. The women stand for a moment before entering. Consuelo knocks and a stern voice authorizes them to enter.

4

Doña Santos comes from a lineage of wealthy people. She often boasts that her bloodline is a direct descendent of the kings and queens of Europe. It was mere curiosity and adventure that brought her relatives to the Americas. Doña Santos sits comfortably sipping her coffee, enjoying the garden outside. Clarissa cannot help but stare at Doña Santos beauty; despite her age. She moves like a bird that flies with suaveness over the sky.

"Consuelo, bring the girl over to see closer." She continues to leisurely drink her coffee. Clarissa is petrified of Doña Santos. It is difficult to comprehend how someone so lovely can be so cold. Doña Santos inspects Clarissa from head to toe. "What is your name girl?"

She hesitates before answering. "Clarissa."

Doña Santos eyebrows arch as she places the cup down. She releases a cynical laugh, "It is amusing to see how forward your mother was to name you such a name. It really is unfitting for a girl of your station. It really was not smart; nevertheless she has been in my service for some time. She is a hard worker."

Dislike rises within Clarissa's stomach. How cruel of Doña Santos to offend her mother for giving her a lovely name. She holds her tongue despite her desire to say something. Doña Santos makes a point to stress the difference in social class. She feels her servants need to know their place. The idea of a servant girl parading around with a name like Clarissa is not palatable to her. If it were not for her parent's loyal steadfast hard work, Doña Santos would have no qualms in letting her go.

"We expect my son tomorrow with guests. We will be preparing a huge party. Consuelo, I have decided that she will do best in the kitchen. You are dismissed!"

Consuelo quietly takes Clarissa by the arm and leaves the draftiness of the room. She is hurt by Doña Santos contempt to her. It is by the grace of her parents she is given a job. Consuelo looks at the poor girl. "Clarissa, do not worry. The kitchen is fun and that is where I work. I will be able to look after you."

Clarissa stands silent.

"Don't worry; you will see your mother soon."

"Consuelo?" with concern in her voice, "Can I expect the rest of the family to be like Doña Santos?"

Consuelo attempts to ease her anxiety. "The Santos family prefers the distinction between rich and poor. Their lives are motivated differently from us. You must never covet the rich for it only brings tragedy and sadness. We come only to work here but our lives lie behind those gates outside of this house."

Clarissa contemplates the disparities that lie between people.

They head to the servant quarters, small rooms away from the big house and located by the stalls. They see Guadalupe heading toward them with a quiet smile. Clarissa feels she has disappointed her by not making a better impression on the Patrones. Guadalupe sees by their demeanor that the experience with Doña Santos did not go as anticipated.

"Consuelo, I see you have been keeping my child company and bringing her to get her uniform." She brushes Clarissa's face with her hand tenderly.

Consuelo remarks quietly, "Clarissa did very well today. She will be working in the kitchen with me."

Guadalupe smiles at Clarissa. "I am glad to hear she will be with you." She gives her daughter a hug. "Clarissa one must be strong and concentrate on doing a good job." She says nothing as she walks along with her mother and Consuelo. This is the first time she understands how hard her parents work and the hardships they endure. Guadalupe has an incredible manner; she carries herself so calmly despite everything. Clarissa is resolved to do her best to make her parents proud.

The large kitchen is made of colorful mosaic art with two great clay ovens. The smell of fresh baked bread permeates the whole place. The room is filled with all sorts of spices from garlic braids to chili peppers tied in strings. There is much congestion in the kitchen, in preparation for tomorrow's festivities. The kitchen staff prepares sauces for the meals at the large center table. Consuelo introduces Clarissa to everyone. Clarissa is familiar with most of the people either from church or town. She feels comfortable in this place where she is welcome.

Consuelo continues to show her about the kitchen. She is impressed by the child's unusual beauty. "You are a pretty girl to be working in a place like this. I wonder?" Clarissa does not know what to think about the remark. "I will look after you as if you were my niece. I have no children or husband. I would like you to be at home with me; like an aunt."

Traces of regret color Consuelo's eyes despite her humor and laughter; the sadness of an empty womb with no nest to be made with love. Maybe it is that Guadalupe and Consuelo are around the same age that it is easy to adopt Clarissa like her own daughter. Clarissa finds Consuelo charming and sweet. The fact that her mother respects her is important to her.

23

"Thank you Consuelo for all your attention and making this day easier."
Consuelo smiles and holds her hesitations of what awaits this pretty girl in
a household full of young men.

Consuelo gets the moncajete from the bottom cupboard, a rock bowl
used to crush down spices into sauces. She asks Clarissa to unbraid the
peppers from the string. There is a large plate rack over the fire where
she places the peppers to toast.

Soledad walks into the kitchen briskly and is not amused with Clarissa's
presence. "Consuelo, why is this girl in the kitchen?"

She informs her that Doña Santos has assigned her to the kitchen.
"Clarissa is Guadalupe's daughter and a lovely girl."

Soledad turns to Clarissa with resentment and exits the kitchen as briskly
as she came in.

Consuelo turns to Clarissa who is uneasy at what has taken place. "She
feels threatened by you, just ignore her, she will have to get over it."

As Clarissa removes the toasted peppers, she is saddened by Soledad's
reaction. The day is already full of mixed experiences.

Consuelo interrupts her thoughts. "I have a small worry about tomorrow
night." She hesitates to tell her but feels it necessary. "It is your first day
working among these people. It is just that some may want to take
liberties especially where a beautiful girl is concerned."

Clarissa listens to her attentively as Consuelo places more peppers on the
plate to toast.

"Tomorrow El Joven Luis Andres will bring some friends, single
bachelors, to this house. I have lived enough to see many pretty girls such
as you, be cursed by them." Consuelo takes the peppers from the plate
and places them in the moncajete bowl. She crushes them with the stone.

"I am sorry to worry you; it is just that you must be careful child. There will be times in which neither your parents nor I will be present to offer you assistance."

Clarissa gives her small green tomatoes to add to the crushing swing of the stone in the moncajete. After they complete the sauce they place it in a dish bathed in blue with drawn white doves outlined in soft gold on the exterior of the dish and cover it. Consuelo walks her to the living room and the open gardens where all the entertainment will be held. They go through the corridor that leads to the tables in which they will be serving the party guests.

The living room is lavish with fine chairs dressed in exquisite ornate designs on soft material. A dynamic fusion of artwork that compliments the masterful carved table, with sculpted vases depicting nature. The color styles range from deep burgundies to fine gold subtleties. It takes her breath away to see such valuables. Clarissa smiles at Soledad who is organizing the tables in hopes to amend the friction between them. Instead, upon their arrival, Soledad gives a grunt of disgust and departs the room. Clarissa follows her with her eyes in sadness. She is unaware of what stands in the room until Consuelo points it out.

Clarissa's eyes ascend to the frame hanging on the wall in a stately manner. Her heart stands still, transfixed by the image before her. It is the most beautiful sight she had ever seen. His eyes have such penetrating presence. It appears that he is looking back at her.

Consuelo is not at all surprised by her admiration of the painting. "The painting of El Joven Luis Andres arrived a few weeks ago from Europe. Doña Santos had the painting commissioned while on a visit. The boy is handsome. Is he not?"

Clarissa is embarrassed that she had been caught staring with intense interest.

Soledad walks into the room laughing at Clarissa. "Have we forgotten our place in this house? As if the Patrones' son could fall for a poor kitchen maid. That is what you are, only good enough to help in the kitchen."

Clarissa feels the blood rush to her tongue. "The malice in your words is a reflection of the dark in your heart. Maybe it is your own feelings being projected because you too are a poor servant." Soledad says nothing to her rebuttal and leaves the room. Clarissa sighs a deep regret. "I am sorry Consuelo. I am sure that she has gone and told Doña Santos. My parents will be so disappointed."

A hearty laugh escapes Consuelo. "You put her in her place and well deserved. Do not concern yourself with her. Doña Santos dislikes problems among servitude. She quickly lets them go before listening to gossip."

Consuelo changes the subject as she notices Clarissa stealing glances of the portrait. "Clarissa, it is obvious the painting has enchanted you. The real thing is more dangerous. He is nothing like this reflection, so quiet and unobtrusive." She gently touches Clarissa's shoulders as they both stare at the picture. "Be extremely careful not to expose what I see in your eyes. It is too dangerous for you and your family. You are such a pretty girl. If you were rich you could aspire to such love but you are poor ... and worse, innocent for that matter."

Clarissa looks away from Consuelo and the portrait with his image already imprinted in her mind. "I would never do anything to disgrace myself or family."

Consuelo sighs as she looks at Clarissa pensively. "I know you will not. It is he I worry about. Doña Santos is very delicate about her son. She adores the boy profusely. Who knows what she has in mind now that he has returned for good." Consuelo remembering her duties interrupts her own talking. "Enough of my jabbering, come we must finish up."

Clarissa follows her, but not before stealing a last glimpse at the portrait as she exits the magnificent room.

5

The major party preparations are complete. Guadalupe comes to take her daughter to the servant quarters for the night. Most of the servants are to stay over at the quarters for the festivities at the big house. Consuelo volunteers to join them since her room is next door. They walk outside in the warm night. Clarissa holds her mother's hand, happy to see her again and inquires about her father. She informs her that she will not see him until late tomorrow.

As they approach the room, the sound of a whip can be heard tearing flesh. A man releases the sound of pure agony while trying to hold what little dignity he has. An overseer whips him by command of the Patrones. Don Santos is upset that he lost a cow due to what he calls the older man's negligence. The overseer abuses his power as he continues beating him. The rhythm strikes his body cutting through his spirit. "Do you know how much it will cost the Patrones to replace this dead animal?" He points at the dead carcass that got stuck in the wires and strangled itself.

The man, with little breath left, apologizes. "I am sorry. It was an accident. I tried to get the animal out."

The satisfaction of watching this man willing to submit to the many lashes; rather than be fired, is justice to Don Santos, who does not stay to administer the judgment. The pelted scars left on his back will become permanent as the blood streams down his back. The old man's fate could have been worse. Don Santos believes himself to be a benevolent man. He could have killed the peasant or fired the family into starvation as others have done.

The overseer looks at the man with little expression and walks away, not before demanding he bury the animal.

The women stand quietly so not to be noticed. Clarissa holds her mother's hand as the shrieks come from the wounded man, an abhorrent noise that moves through the soul. It is rare these horrendous things happen in the Hacienda. Guadalupe tries to shield Clarissa from the anguish the poor man suffers. Consuelo nods empathetically, aware that the poor person is lying in the puddle of his blood. They see the overseer walk out of the stall, wiping the stain from his whip with a cloth.

They wait patiently before Consuelo speaks out loud. "I heard Don Santos speak with his wife that one of his animals died. He was upset and was going to seriously deal with the matter."

Guadalupe moves her head in regret for the poor man, knowing it could be easily her husband lying there in his place. Clarissa is stricken with sadness, knowing an individual could inflict such pain on a weak man. The cruelty of the rich made little sense when they had everything; yet they forfeit a person's spirit so easily.

"We must help him Mama."

Guadalupe and Consuelo know that they have to be careful not to be caught by the overseer or the Patrones. "I will go to the kitchen and prepare something to help restore some of his strength."

Guadalupe agrees and Consuelo leaves quickly. Guadalupe holds her daughter's hand as they move away from the stalls and head to the gardens. They follow a dark and inauspicious path, heading to the rustic gardens made of desert flowers, cactuses and aloe vera plants. Clarissa stands close to her mother who carefully chooses the aloe plant that would not be noticed if gone. It is oozing with yellow medicinal, curative properties and wicked when pricked by this plant. After cutting a few leaves they slowly walk to the stalls. Consuelo arrives with a bowl of soup and a bucket of water. They step in silence, fearful of what they would find inside.

The smell of dead animal penetrates the entire stall. The shape of what seems an amorphous figure crouches, trying to get up. The blood around him marks the floor. Clarissa takes this in, unable to understand. The women move toward the man. He is trying to get the strength to stand up and bury the animal, laying a few steps away from him. The flies dance around the carcass a horrible sight. On his back is a map of sorrow and misfortune in the scars. Guadalupe uses her apron and pours water, as she carefully cleans the blood. The poor man crouches weeping softly by the generosity of the women. They speak very little as to respect the dignity of a torn man. Clarissa offers the broth to sip. He struggles to swallow the liquid from the bowl that lands on his already soiled shirt.

Guadalupe instructs the old man to stay still. "We need you to lie on your stomach; we are going to put some medicine on your back." The man objects profusely but his strength extinguishes. He lies on the earth motionless. "We will bury the animal while Clarissa places the medicine."

Consuelo stands and follows Guadalupe to the animal. The pestilence is potent yet somehow these women grab the heavy animal and drag it out to be buried. They are strong, molded for hard labor. It is the only way to survive when things find themselves difficult. The stakes are too high for this particular incident especially since they are now involved.

Clarissa bends next to the man with his eyes closed in slumber. She hums quietly to ease his pain. She hopes her music transfers his mind elsewhere, to a place of peace. The women come back with the signature of the animal blood over their clothing. They place the shovel next to him. Consuelo has lemons to remove any trace of the animal's smell on them. Clarissa is proud of these women who demonstrate such ability to take control of this abhorrent situation. She removes the aloe leaves from his back carefully so as to not interrupt his slumber. They depart from the stalls carefully, walking away and turning once to see the poor man absorbed by the darkness of this place. It is all they could do to help.

6

The smell of the kitchen is wonderful. It is hard to imagine that the night before had been so difficult. The preparations for the festivities are set. The chickens, marinated in spices, are roasting slowly. The dough is set to put into the adobe ovens. The cactus salad, which was introduced to Doña Santos by Guadalupe; prepared cold with cilantro, minced Serrano peppers, tomatoes, onions and tender cactuses, is chilling. The cheeses, freshly prepared from goat's milk. The soup is comprised of a delightful blend of squash. The sweet decadent desserts are ready: an assortment of flans, tier cakes of all flavors and specialized fruit candies, as well as imported chocolates detailed with flowers and birds. The decoration of flowers, musicians and hired help move to a quick beat of a drum. The place comes together with live spirits. The servants are ready and dressed for work. Clarissa is assisting Consuelo with the last preparations for the party. Doña Santos is inspecting the house ensuring everything is in order. The excitement escalates throughout the house as the dinner hour approaches. Clarissa is in the kitchen alone while Consuelo steps out for a moment. It is not long before she rushes in to advise Clarissa that the guest of honor has arrived.

"They have arrived! El Joven Luis Andres and his party have arrived and are outside. The boy looks beautiful."

Consuelo holds her chest, gasping for air. Clarissa stops what she is doing and moves toward Consuelo. She takes Clarissa by the hand and rushes her outside through the bushes not to be seen. They see him descend from the carriage like a proud peacock in splendor. Clarissa's heart drops at the sight of the young and elegant man. The other men accompanying him are handsome as well. Luis Andres de los Santos is indeed more beautiful than his portrait. They laugh heartily among each other as Doña Santos in tears, content to know that her only child is home. Her beloved son embraces and kisses her tenderly on her cheek. Don Santos stands austere and simply nods his head and walks into the house. Doña Santos holds his arms and leads them all into the house.

Clarissa feels embarrassed to be there, watching them in secrecy. She pulls on Consuelo's sleeve. "Consuelo let us go inside. If my mother sees me here, I hate to imagine what she may think."

Consuelo interrupts, "Your mother went home. Doña Santos was in an excellent mood and let her go home early. She was looking for you but I told her not to worry. It is good for her to take a break when she can. Also Roberto will be picking you up later tonight."

They walk toward the kitchen when they see everyone is inside.

Doña Santos embraces her child's arm with great delight.

Don Santos is proud of his son, despite his conservative affections to him. "We prepared quite a party and dancing too." He heads toward his son and gives him a hard embrace. "I am glad you are home. It is now time to take care of things here."

Luis Andres looks at his father and says nothing. Don Santos invites all the young men to drink a glass of brandy. They follow him to the study.

Doña Santos holds her son and whispers to him, "Aimee is coming tonight. She looks forward to seeing you my son. Luis Andres, she is a beautiful creature and properly brought up. It would make your father and I so happy to see you wed."

Luis Andres listens to her attentively. He humors her as he tries to unleash his hand softly to follow his friends. "Yes, mother I look forward to seeing how Aimee has turned out. Do not worry for tonight. I will look for her." He had a weakness for women. He remembers Aimee as a lovely child and is curious to know how the sweet flower has bloomed since his departure. Luis Andres kisses his mother and walks toward the study with the other men.

Over fifty small-basted hens are prepared for the mole dish. The exotic dish is a favorite of Luis Andres. The legend of its creation is attributed to a concoction that nuns created in desperation of the unexpected visit from the Archbishop. It is said they used all the spices in the cupboard to create the spicy chocolate sauce.

All the servants are in serving attire for the party. Doña Santos has instructed to not see anyone in two braids. She thinks it is a way to appear less provincial and more sophisticated. Clarissa is uneasy and stays close to Consuelo. Everyone in the household is prepared to attend to the arriving guests. Consuelo smiles at Clarissa and wonders if she has any idea what a lovely child she is despite her servant outfit. Doña Santos walks to the kitchen to ensure that everything is ready for serving. She moves arrogantly and quickly glances at Clarissa. Doña Santos thinks for a moment that Clarissa may be too distracting to the guests especially among the men but quickly dismisses the thought. Clarissa looks at the ground trying to make as little contact as possible for it is apparent that Doña Santos does not fancy her. She has to be careful not to offend her.

At that moment, Soledad rushes into the kitchen and moves to Doña Santos out of breathe. "Doña Santos. La Nina Aimee and her family are here."

The news brightens her disposition and flippantly gives her orders to start serving as she heads out the kitchen with Soledad following after her.

A few minutes later, music is heard as soft voices merge together in harmony through the house as if in a lovely dream. Consuelo places her hand on Clarissa's shoulder to assure her everything is going to be fine, well aware of the anxiety she is feeling. "Stay close to me Clarissa." She smiles. "Let us take these plates before Doña Santos or Soledad comes in screaming like a cat."

The plates are decorated with geometric fruit carvings with the center consisting of small pastries that tempt the palate. They take the plates to their appointed destination. They proceed through the door of the kitchen into open territory. Clarissa, behind Consuelo, follows like a dart not losing her target. The music begins to crescendo as they get closer and closer to the living room. The sudden brightness of the room lets her know they have arrived. The voices are soft harmonious to the music. She hears the laughter and murmuring of people. They travel to the table set earlier with flowers. It is through the peripheral of her eye she sees the elegance of the people present. Clarissa had never seen such fashionable wear, it is breathtaking. A young lady next to Doña Santos catches her attention. Clarissa, unaware and distracted, hits Consuelo with the plate. Nothing falls.

"Clarissa, do not draw attention child." She moves closer to Consuelo and apologizes.

"I am sorry. I will be more careful."

Consuelo nods as they place the plates down on the table. At that moment they clearly hear the voice a young man laughing as they look up from the table. She feels the warmth rise to her cheeks. Adjacent to the table stands El Joven Luis Andres smiling attentively. Clarissa puts her head down immediately, walks toward the kitchen, forgetting Consuelo.

7

Doña Santos is ecstatic at the sight of Aimee de la Madrid. She is the young lady that will marry her beloved son Luis Andres. She has bloomed into a jewel of perfection with fine graces and discriminating taste. Her family is one of the most respected and prominent families in Mexico City. Their fortune is equal to the Santos family. The arrangement of both families united through matrimony would bring great wealth, power and happiness to both the Santos and De La Madrid family.

The first sight of Luis Andres was an inner delight for Aimee. She is confident knowing she is the most handsome woman in the room. Luis Andres' time of frolicking abroad is over and it is time for him to settle, she thought. They were ideal; both full of vanity and fortune. They would be the new breed of elite socialites in Mexico. Luis Andres excuses himself from his friends and walks slowly across the room with a smirk of assurance on his face. He is a man who loves beautiful things. Aimee de la Madrid is very striking and to be appreciated. His companions are very much taken by her beauty. Luis Andres bows his head, looks up and gives her a mischievous look.

"Luis Andres, is Aimee not the loveliest thing you have ever seen? I expect both of you to reacquaint yourselves." Doña Santos looks at

Aimee with satisfaction at the sight of them together. "I will leave you both together and seek out your father."

After Doña Santos departure, he takes her hand gently kisses it. "It is indeed a pleasant surprise Aimee."

She smiles sweetly. 'I have been looking forward to seeing you again my dear Luis Andres." She looks toward the direction of his friends who are watching them attentively. "Are you not going to introduce me to your friends?"

He smirks at the request and gives his arm out and escorts her to them. He starts with his French import and best friend Jean-Claude Tusset, who is impressed by her beauty. "Enchante, Mademoiselle Aimee."

Aimee feasts on the admiration and responds graciously to his compliment.

Luis Andres finds his friend's reaction very entertaining. He continues with the introduction of Alexis Ferrel, unaware they had met at a social gathering in Mexico City. Alexis is acquainted with the family and had hopes to court her himself, an unpleasant surprise he tries to conceal. It would be difficult to compete with Luis Andres for the affection of Aimee.

Alexis moves to kiss her hand. "Senorita De La Madrid, what a pleasure to see you again. I had no idea you knew Luis Andres and his family?"

"So, you have met before. Should I be jealous?" Luis Andres raises his eyebrow in interest.

"No need to be jealous. We are simply acquaintances that met at a party." Alexis feels a blow to his heart and ego. They had met at other parties and she was attentive to him. However, here she is a different creature with a different agenda. He attempts to rekindle something with her other than civility. "You must promise me at least one dance tonight, for a friend."

Aimee does not like the manner in which he baits her. She stares at Luis Andres and politely states, "Only if Luis Andres permits it."

The remarks cause the men to break out in a laugh.

Alexis holds his embarrassment and gives into the laugh himself. "Indeed, I would not like to monopolize your time. There are other lovely women in the room, just look at the servant girl with the plate."

Aimee does not receive the remark well, despite her smile. Luis Andres looks toward the direction of the servant girl placing the plate on the table. He is somehow magnetized by her presence. The sight of pure heaven incarnate in body that swayed seductively in her innocence. At that moment he blocks everything except Clarissa. Alexis is busy reacting to Aimee who is not pleased by the comparison to a servant girl. He meant to hurt her pride and succeeded. Aimee is upset for a second that she fails to notice Luis Andres' distraction. Jean-Claude was enraptured by the simplicity of such beauty. The young girl aware looks momentarily at Luis Andres then looks down and quickly leaves the room. Luis Andres follows her until she is gone.

Jean-Claude seems to read his friend's thoughts. He speaks under his breath as he remarks, "She is lovely."

"I must say I have never seen anyone with her kind of beauty." Luis Andres replies, courteously, "Indeed she is uncommonly pretty for a servant girl. But she is merely a servant."

Jean-Claude understands the ramification behind his remark. His friend would never marry below his station despite any great temptation. However this imposed another possibility that was common for men of wealth. They could have a lovely past time set aside in the oblivion of darkness.

Aimee's curiosity is peaked by the exchange of quiet words between Luis Andres and Jean-Claude. "I hope I am not intruding?"

Luis Andres with knowing suspicion, "We were just commenting how blessed we are with the presence of such exquisite loveliness." Aimee places her hand around his arm.

Jean-Claude interrupts, "I hope you permit moi a dance?"

She stares into Luis Andres eyes with a seductive look, "But of course."

Luis Andres gently gets her hand and kisses it softly as he gives her a mischievous gleam.

8

In the kitchen Clarissa is still blushing with heightened nerves. Consuelo tries to ease her anxiety by embracing her fear away. She is shivering in discomfort. "Consuelo, I cannot sweep this uncomfortable feeling."

She is about to say something when Soledad walks in irritated to find them in the kitchen. "What are we doing standing around when there are guests to be served. Have you forgotten your station in this house or must I remind you?" Soledad's venom falls easily from her lips. "Consuelo, make sure she does not ruin tonight," and walks away.

Although Clarissa is bothered by her words she understands she cannot do anything to change her way.

Consuelo is preoccupied with the observation of how young men look at Clarissa. It is something she does not like at all. She speaks seriously to her, "Be careful my child, with these people. They perceive life differently than us. Although they may be draped in fine luxuries, we are clothed in finer qualities that are not so visible. Do not allow temptation to blind your truth."

Clarissa heeds her words of advice. "Thank you Consuelo for your attentions."

Consuelo is deeply touched by the girl's genuine sweetness. "Come Clarissa; let us finish serving the guests. Stay close behind me."

They both give out a small laugh. Although she is anxious, Clarissa manages to push distracting thoughts to her deepest part. It is now time to serve the dinner. Soledad directs each of the girls to their assigned table. Clarissa is hoping not to get Luis Andres' table but is purposely assigned by Soledad. It is her desire that Clarissa make a nervous mistake leading to her termination. This is a very important event for the Santos family and they will not tolerate any mistakes. Consuelo glares at the mean-spirited Soledad. Clarissa resumes staying focused on doing her job well. She is not going to allow anything to interfere. Clarissa approaches the table unaware of how lovely she looks. It is easier for Clarissa to place the plates down while Consuelo serves the sauce over the dinner if requested. Luis Andres and his friends notice her approaching but continue with the conversation at hand. She places the first setting for Alexis, unsuspecting of his hand taking the liberty of pinching her behind. Consuelo holding the sauce bowl is not aware of the stray hand that has violated Clarissa. Alexis has taken the privilege to offend her while serving. There is an ignited fire in her eyes as she tries to compose herself without bringing attention to herself. She swiftly moves away not offering him the sauce that Consuelo was holding.

Alexis finds new amusement in this poor girl. He wants to provoke the situation further. "Girl, you forget to offer the sauce for my dinner."

Clarissa feels her anger pulsing but says nothing. In subtle retaliation, Clarissa is drowning his dinner in the sauce and moves forward. They laugh at what seems is the expense of her humiliation. It is Consuelo who gives her the courage to override the incident and continue.

Luis Andres observes her reaction and makes light of the situation, "Alexis, the sauce will be to your liking."

Alexis understood he is to behave and not start any mishap. Clarissa quietly serves Jean-Claude who apologizes for his friend's behavior. She looks into his eyes and sees sincerity and gives a quick nod in acceptance. Jean-Claude is amazed by the power those large brown eyes can have on a person. They had been blazing in anger and quickly put to calm by an apology. Luis Andres notices his friend's interaction with the servant girl as he sips his drink.

The moment had come to serve Luis Andres. Clarissa feels the tightness of her stomach as she approaches him. He moves close to her as she places the plate down. She hears his breath next to her as he thanks her. She maintains control despite the desire of her body to combust into many stars of brightness. Luis Andres finds himself hypnotized by the girl such that he forgets he is being watched by his friends, including Aimee. He has known many women in his life but none that could stir such uneasiness. Luis Andres finds Clarissa beguiling. It is the beauty and innocence embodied in simplicity that attracts him. He has the ability to restrain himself from many women he had encountered in his lifetime. Clarissa is different.

Alexis erupts in laughter at the witness of such a tender moment between Luis Andres and the servant girl. At the realization of his transfixed look, he abruptly turns away. Aimee is not content with the presence of the girl serving their table. Clarissa, confused and flustered, tries to focus on the task at hand. The voice of Luis Andres, soft and soothing, moves like a song that enraptures the blood with a tingling sensation. She dares not look at his eyes. Clarissa is fearful of those around, yet more of Luis Andres. She places the plate down for Aimee who is steaming to release her dislike. It was to be her night and no peasant was going to overshadow her attentions.

"It is hard to find good help. Not every peasant with braids can serve. It is even worse if you have to remind them of their place. In my house they know their place and the consequences should they forget."

Alexis enjoys the entire scene unfolding, especially the apparent jealousy of Aimee to the girl. Clarissa is mortified by her unkind comments and simply places the plate with her head down and goes away from the table. Consuelo wants to drown her in the sauce for those malicious words. The day is proving to be difficult by the added insults of Aimee.

On the other hand Aimee is amused to see her depart. "These servants of your mother are prideful, imagine that. They do not wait until they are excused."

Luis Andres is serious as he watches them depart. He stares at Aimee with a critical eye. "Aimee that was not very ladylike. You are worse than Alexis."

Aimee grabs his hand and softly whispers in his ear, "My darling Luis Andres. I am beginning to think you prefer the hired help over my presence."

Annoyed by her suggestion, he takes his arm away and holds his glass of wine. He moves the conversation toward enjoying the food and wonderful company. They all raise their glasses in agreement. Aimee, satisfied to know that Luis Andres is particular about the people he is around as she was, holds her glass with enjoyment.

9

Clarissa walks briskly to the kitchen holding back all the feelings swelling within her disillusioned heart. Consuelo follows struggling to match her pace. When they arrive in the kitchen, Clarissa rests her hands on the table with tears resting on her cheeks. She breaths as Consuelo watches helpless. "How could they? How could people that look so fine be so cruel?"

Consuelo unaware that she was thinking out loud responded softly, "The arrogance of wealth makes those less fortunate vulnerable to cruelty." Clarissa is suffering. She is not prepared to handle the indiscretion of the rich. Consuelo makes her sit down and brings her some water. Clarissa's fears are being realized. This is no place for her. It will bring her misery.

"Oh Consuelo, I am trying to not be affected, but I cannot anymore." Her tears came streaming down her face. "You saw what happened." She continues to sob. "I do not deserve this treatment from them. I was doing my work."

Consuelo, moved by her grief, attempts to console her by holding her as a child. "My dear girl the night is almost done. Tonight will be your last day working here. I have a cousin who owns a bakery and needs help in his shop. I will speak with your parents and arrange for you to work there." She holds her and thinks of the pain of her empty womb. It could easily be her daughter shedding these tears. She will do her best to lead the girl away from danger. "Now child, dry those tears. After tonight you will never have to see these horrible people again."

Clarissa smiles and is better at leaving this antagonistic place. Her only regret is not seeing Luis Andres again.

Soledad comes into the kitchen upset, looking for Consuelo. She ignores Clarissa completely. "Doña Santos wants to see you now!"

Consuelo follows but not before instructing Clarissa to start cleaning the kitchen.

Alexis is stung by the charm of the servant girl and hopes by the end of the night to be more closely acquainted. He waits for the proper opportunity as they advance outside to enjoy the dance and music. Alexis takes advantage that Aimee is clinging to Luis Andres and focused elsewhere. "Luis Andres, I left something inside. I will be back."

Luis Andres knows exactly what he is scheming. "I am sure Alexis that it could wait until later."

Jean-Claude comments whimsically, "Women are like lovely birds. There is much fun here to have. Look at all the lovely birds with great plumage."

Alexis, determined to spite his friends responds cynically, "I enjoy more domestic birds. I find they make for the most delightful caged pets. After they have lost their charm I simply release them."

Luis Andres is not happy with his last remark. "I find that certain birds will not be easily caught."

"Luis Andres, do you feel the bird is better off with another owner?"

Aimee, annoyed with Alexis' conversation, interrupts, "I am bored with all this talk about birds." She looks directly at Alexis as she holds Luis Andres arm tightly, "Alexis, do whatever you have to do, but leave Luis Andres out of it." She moves close to Luis Andres with her sweet intoxicating perfume. "The music is delightful, let us dance."

Although his thoughts are with Alexis' intentions, the seduction before him is difficult to resist. He gently kisses her hand and consents to the dance floor.

Alexis finds the kitchen with no problem; he simply allows his nose to lead the way. He is fortunate to find Clarissa alone facing away from the entrance. He walks slowly, measuring his steps so she does not notice him yet. He startles her by placing his hand around her waist.

Clarissa leaps instantly and successfully untangles herself from his grip. She tries to reserve her composure as she speaks to him. "How can I help you Joven?"

He gazes at her with lecherous pretenses as he tries to get close to her. "I want you to stop what you are doing and join me for a nice walk."

Clarissa moves away from his every approach. The fear takes over as she pleads softly to be left alone to do her work. "Please leave me to my work." Her voice breaks revealing her terror. She looks to the door hoping Consuelo will walk in. Even Soledad would be welcomed. Clarissa is vulnerable to the man who assaulted her earlier. She feels abhorrence for this person who has invaded her security. She takes the rock from the moncajete, used earlier to crush peppers into a sauce. It is her source of defense.

Clarissa tries to reason with him. "Please, I must attend to my work." She holds the rock upward, serious about using it if needed.

Alexis finds it entertaining; the use of a mere stone to defend herself from his desires. He laughs heartily. "You are more irresistible than any imaginable nymph. Why are you being so cruel? I can offer you a better world than just serving. You would be my woman only."

Clarissa is disgusted by his insinuations. "I am a descent person, I would never. I implore you in the name of God please leave me alone!"

Alexis thrives at the range of emotions displayed by his taunting. She moves toward the table as to secure a separation between them. He seductively walks toward her, not caring for her idle threats. "I love a feisty woman for it is sweeter when I make her docile."

Clarissa, well aware that she could not scream without bringing grave consequences to her parents, hopes that Consuelo will come before anything horrible can happen to her. The table will not be able to keep the proximity between them for long.

In an unexpected move Alexis is able to get her hand, not before she swings and hits his lips. He can taste his blood from the small opening of the lip that had been parted by the rock in her hand. Upset he pins both her hands in his and caresses her with his bloody lips.

Terrified, Clarissa struggles to free herself, pleading in tears.

Doña Santos calls Consuelo and is upset by what Aimee had mentioned about Clarissa. It is bad behavior not to excuse oneself from serving a table, especially with an important guest like Aimee. She knows Doña Santos was going to be severe with her. She waits patiently as Don and Doña Santos look with satisfaction at the union of her son and Aimee. They dance with repose and elegance. Doña Santos waits until the dance is finished to call her over. Aimee excuses herself from Luis Andres despite not wanting to leave his side. However, she knows that her future in-laws will be the key in making their union permanent. It is wonderful to be the envy of everyone.

Don Santos is pleased with Aimee and not able to hold his compliment. "Aimee, you are a true vision of loveliness."

Doña Santos gives Aimee a sweet kiss on the cheek. "I must agree with my husband. I dare say you will make an ideal wife and mistress of this house one day."

Aimee humbly smiles. "You are too kind to me and truly I cannot wait to be a part of this family."

Don Andres walks away and leaves the ladies to talk.

"My dearest Aimee, I apologize for the indiscretion of my servants. It is difficult to find good help."

Aimee listens attentively as she watches Luis Andres and Jean-Claude step inside.

Doña Santos notices Aimee's interest and offers her a word of advice. "Aimee dearest, men will be men. Do not worry where my son is at all times. The important thing is that you will be his wife." She smiles in unison with her.

Doña Santos turns her attention to Consuelo, who was forced to hear everything. "Consuelo, the next time you offend any of my guests it will cost you dearly. Aimee will one day be the mistress of this house and it will be your obligation to treat her with utmost respect. This is a warning Consuelo. Remember I can replace any of you at any time. Also let Guadalupe's daughter know that she will not work out. You can depart now."

Aimee is content to know that the servant girl will be let go.

Jean-Claude notices that Alexis has not returned. His thoughts go quickly to the poor girl who had served them. Alexis loves exploiting, especially susceptible girls. After his dance with Aimee, Luis Andres goes inside. It bothers him that Alexis could be doing something stupid to this girl. Luis Andres walks briskly toward the kitchen sensing something is not well. As they approach they hear the soft cry of a girl pleading. They both walk into the kitchen and see Clarissa fighting with her assailant who holds her close and ferociously kissing her. Luis Andres snaps, as a volcanic anger erupts into physical violence. He grabs Alexis with his hands and crashes his fist into his mouth. He throws him across the floor, dropping him by the doorway.

Alexis is startled by his reaction. "Estupido! What was that for? I asked if you were interested in *her*?"

Clarissa is visibly shaken.

"How dare you offend my workers? I do not want you to bother her again."

Alexis picks himself up, sweeps the dirt from his clothing, takes his handkerchief from his coat and wipes the blood from his lip. "You surprise me Luis Andres. I thought your tastes were more particular. What would Aimee say about all this?"

Luis Andres speaks sternly to him, "Alexis it is best that you leave the kitchen now. Do not forget you are a guest in my house."

Alexis looks at Clarissa and spits his blood in her direction as he exits the kitchen. Luis Andres takes a handkerchief from his coat and asks Jean-Claude to put water on it. He obediently gets the water from a clay pitcher. Luis Andres hands the cloth to Clarissa who is petrified and embarrassed by Alexis' behavior. Luis Andres is concerned that someone could walk in and see the young girl in her disheveled condition. He hands her the cloth and tries to make small talk in order to make her feel less threatened of them.

"I apologize for my friend's horrible conduct. We are not all like him. Can I ask what your name is?"

Clarissa, trying to regain her composure, shyly responds. "My name is Clarissa."

They are astounded by the nature of her name for it was uncustomary for a servant to hold such a name. He speaks softly to her. "Clarissa, you must not allow anyone to see you like this." He gently touches her shoulder, causing her to jump away from him. This touch sends a shiver through her body, so unfamiliar it scares her. He understands her natural reaction to him.

Clarissa, aware of her situation, is trying hard to get a hold of her thoughts. Luis Andres is the last person she would want to see her in such a deplorable situation. Yet were it not for him, who would have saved her from the despicable monster forcing himself on her.

Luis Andres stands patiently as he speaks to her with gentleness. "I promise he will never bother you again. I give you the word of a gentleman."

She releases a sigh, tainted with sorrow. She lifts her head and thanks them both through her teary eyes. Jean Claude unnaturally extends his hand and introduces himself and offers his assistance. She gives a sweet smile that makes Luis Andres envious of his friend. He waits for Jean-Claude to finish his introduction before extending his hand to her. He unexpectedly kisses her hand, which shocks Clarissa; who stands watching him before moving her hand away.

Clarissa moves away from them not knowing what to expect. Luis Andres is beautiful in her eyes, she feels it best not to stare but look at the ground with periodic acknowledgment to his friend who also was handsome. Her thought is lost in confusion over everything. Clarissa's heart is beating so fast she dreads her emotions are translucent for him to read. She does not want to show any indication of what he is making her feel inside. She tries hard to resume her work by assuring them she is well now.

"Thank you for your concern. I am very grateful to you gentlemen. However your guests will find it strange you are in the kitchen with the help, so please go." It is incredible she found the strength to ask them to leave the kitchen. They both understand it would not help her situation if they found them in the kitchen with her.

"We will depart Clarissa. I promise to look after you so no harm will follow such a lovely girl such as yourself," stated Luis Andres as he moves close to her for a moment. She quickly gives him back his handkerchief. Luis Andres nods as he takes hold of her hand gently that holds the cloth. "I beg you to please hold on to it."

Jean-Claude observes his friend with interest as he interacts with the servant girl. It is uncommon for him to display such sincerity of affection to someone like Clarissa. They both bow their head and leave the kitchen.

Consuelo walks into the kitchen and is stunned to find them there.

They nod with a smile and depart.

10

Consuelo goes to Clarissa to question her about their visit to the kitchen. She breaks down in tears and narrates the horrible events before their arrival. Consuelo is mortified, as her face turns pale with aggravation by the details. "I expected something like this but not so soon." Her thoughts are consumed with Doña Santos remarks of wanting her out of the house today. It is not in Clarissa's interest to stay in this place any longer. It is better this way for her to start elsewhere, away from temptation and the danger this place extends. "Clarissa, do not worry any longer as I have said before you will start work at the bakery with my cousin. It is best this way so nothing like this happens again. You were very fortunate this time." She hugs her and Clarissa releases the sorrow she is already carrying.

Roberto walks to the door of the kitchen and notices both women embracing. He stands close to the door until he is noticed. There is something not well as he stands in silence. Consuelo looks up and quickly acknowledges the young man watching them attentively. "I have to take Clarissa home."

Consuelo without thinking blurts out, "It is good that she leaves this place, never to come back. This is not a place for a lovely girl such as Clarissa."

Roberto's face is bent with concern as he moves toward Clarissa to discover pain in her face. "Did something happen, Clarissa?"

She moves toward him and places her hand on his arm. "Oh no Roberto, nothing worth remembering." She looks at Consuelo pleading with her eyes not to mention the day's incident.

Roberto stares at Clarissa and sees something that was not there before, a new suffering. He understands not to question her anymore. He is helpless and frustrated at the notion that someone hurt the woman he loves most in the world. They walk out together, holding his arm for refuge against all horrible things she has experienced in that big house.

Consuelo rushes to hug the sweet girl before departing into the carriage with Roberto. Consuelo sees them as a perfect fit. He would be able to protect her from the harshness life sometimes offers. Consuelo waits by the back door of the kitchen. Roberto tenderly helps Clarissa up into the carriage. They move away from the house not looking back. Her eyes cling to the carriage as Clarissa and Roberto disappear in the blue night. Consuelo is relieved to notice how Roberto is completely in love with Clarissa, who seems unaware of his affections. "The boy is in love with her." Consuelo is unaware of the presence behind her.

"Who is in love with whom?"

She is startled to see El Joven Luis Andres in the kitchen again and alone. She struggles to say something coherent.

Luis Andres looks to the direction of the road and notices a carriage far away. He looks around for the girl. "Where is Clarissa?"

Consuelo, perplexed at him, says nothing. He repeats the question again to her more sternly with anxiousness in his voice this time. She points out to the shadow of the carriage. He walks out slowly almost in a trance looking in the direction in silence. Consuelo follows a few steps behind him. "She has left never to come to this house again. It is best for everyone. Do you not agree Joven Luis Andres?"

He stands still a moment longer, watching the parting figure disappear. He turns and looks directly at Consuelo, says nothing and walks away quickly.

Consuelo is left speechless at what she sees in his eyes.

Roberto waits for Clarissa to say something to him but she remains quiet. Clarissa's thoughts are far away from his grasp. He looks at her through the side of his eyes and is convinced something is wrong. He cannot resist any longer and asks her what really took place in the big house. She does not respond to his question. Roberto stops the carriage and gently grabs her arm. She slowly lifts her eyes and reveals her profound sadness enveloped in a tear. His heart aches at this sight. "Clarissa, what happened to you?"

She looks at him tenderly like a child. "Roberto, I just do not understand why people must be cruel. They treat us like we are worth nothing." Roberto embraces her softly as she weeps on his shoulders. "I do not understand how my parents can work for such mean people?"

Roberto speaks to her like a child. "Clarissa, they have no choice. It is obvious how young you are still in the ways of this world." Clarissa says nothing. Roberto realizes it is best to get her home to her parents. He resumes his journey home in the quiet and warm darkness.

Aimee entertains herself with the young men who are flocked around her. However, deep inside, she is upset by the disappearance of Luis Andres and his friend. She wonders what could lure them away from her. She notices that Alexis has come in somewhat disarrayed. She means to approach him but thinks it prudent not to do so, especially since Alexis is vexed by her disinterest in him. Moments later Jean-Claude comes in without Luis Andres. This makes her uncomfortable. Aimee feels something is not right about the entire situation. She wonders if he is exploring the domestic help, specifically that detestable girl. It did not bother her as long as it is just having fun with the hired help, nothing serious. Her thoughts are put to rest as she notices the lovely figure of a man who was none other than Luis Andres. She walks toward him ignoring everything around her. "Luis Andres you have me very neglected."

She places her arm around his. Luis Andres looks at Aimee who is indeed a perfect jewel to be had. Her eyes have a certain mischievousness, desirable to any man including himself. She had a magnifying quality that it is no surprise to find her in the company of many suitors. Her lips are moist like the fruits of summer that taste the sweetest. He kisses her wrist tenderly all the while thinking of Clarissa. Luis Andres is bothered that he missed her although his demeanor displayed a different façade. Aimee moves him toward the dance floor. Luis Andres smiles and takes over the invitation starting the musical pace. They serenade the floor remarkably, capturing the attention of those around. There is both admiration and envy by the spectators present.

Clarissa walks into her small house lit by a candle in the bedroom. Her father Jacinto sleeps on a petate, which is a straw-like mat on the dirt floor of the living room and kitchen. The other room is for her and her mother. Her father constructed a small bed from pieces of wood. Guadalupe is waiting in bed embroidering a shawl. She looks at Clarissa's eyes and knows something has occurred. She walks quietly around her father who lies sleeping. She draws the cloth that serves as a door dividing the living room from the bedroom. Guadalupe's heart swells at the words read by her daughter's simple tears. She wants to provide her only daughter a haven of safety. She wonders for a single moment if it is selfish to bring her life into this difficult world. Yet she could not imagine living a world without her blessed daughter. Guadalupe draws her daughter close letting her weep quietly as she caresses her hair.

"Mi vida you will not have to go back there ever again. All will take care of itself in time." She glances at the small portrait of the Virgin Mary, finding some solace for her daughter.

11

The night before seemed like a dream, as there were only a few traces of last night's party. The house went back to its elegant ways. The servants return to the bustling rhythm of its chores. In the dining table Doña Santos is having breakfast with Aimee. "I will have to replace that pathetic girl. It is a pity she did not turn out like the mother or father. It is apparent she would cause a great deal of problems than she is worth."

Aimee smiles. "I agree completely Doña Santos. She seems like she would definitely bring many problems to this household."

Luis Andres walks in with Jean-Claude catching Aimee's last phrase. "Who is the problem my dearest?"

Doña Santos quickly interrupts to give her beloved son a kiss. "How did you sleep my boy?"

He goes over to greet them with a kiss on the cheek. "Very well mother, now what of this problem?"

Doña Santos is annoyed but consents to tell him. "Well if you must know I was trying out one of the servant's daughter. She just did not work out as well as the parents. The fact that she had a name above her station bothered me. I cannot believe the audacity of Guadalupe to call her daughter Clarissa."

Aimee burst in a small laugh. She finds it humorous that a servant would be so bold as to do such an absurd thing. "How silly of the parents indeed, why not call her Maria or Paquita; something more befitting."

Luis Andres draws a chair next to his friend. He looks at both his mother and Aimee who appear at that moment morbidly unattractive. "Well, maybe Guadalupe wants something better for her daughter."

Dona Santos and Aimee are appalled by his remark.

Doña Santos would not hear of it. "Please, Luis Andres, we all have our status in life. They must learn never to forget who they are and what their purpose in life is."

Jean-Claude stands quiet, observing his friend as he responds irritably. "Mother, the problem is you think the world is made to serve you and your selfish ways."

Doña Santos's voice rises with hostility. "We sent you abroad so you would be more educated. Instead you come back with absurd notions of saving the servitude."

Don Santos walks into the dining table sensing some tension between his son and wife. He is a striking and handsome older man despite his austere appearance. In time Luis Andres would be the splitting image of him. "Luis Andres, what stupidities are you discussing with your mother that has her upset?"

Doña Santos explains, "He would have the servant's revolt against us."

Luis Andres is bothered by his mother gross exaggeration. "Mother please, I just believe that people have the right to dream of a better existence."

Don Santos takes his seat across the table and looks at his son sarcastically. "Yes, as long it does not interfere with our way of life."

Don Santos shared the same belief as his wife. Their music is a distinction of classes. It is the only way to capitalize his family's wealth. Don Santos changes the subject and admires the beauty of Aimee. "We are so fortunate to have in our presence such a lovely flower like Aimee. It makes for an enjoyable meal."

Aimee shyly smiles. "You are too kind Don Santos."

Jean-Claude notices that Luis Andres is not content with his father's way of resolving the conversation but quickly returns to his regular composure as if nothing happened. Jean-Claude is always intrigued by his friend's reclusive nature at times when pertaining to his true person. His interaction with his father was cold and proper, and made him comprehend some of his friend's complexities. Luis Andres is unable to reveal who he really is. He projects what people expect of him, to maintain the social status and prejudices that came with them.

12

"Buenos Dias Guadalupe. It is a fine morning. I have come for your daughter Clarissa." Consuelo finds Guadalupe preparing coffee. "I have to have her meet my cousin Pedro. He is happy to know that he will be getting someone to help him sell bread."

Guadalupe brings her a cup of the brew and smiles gratefully. "Thank you for everything. It is unfortunate it did not work out at the big house of the Patrones."

Consuelo nods her head in agreement. "I think it best. Doña Santos is a difficult woman to work for anyway. Your child would have suffered unnecessarily." Consuelo knows her presence in the house already stirred something in the eyes of El Joven. It is better to keep her away from the lion.

"Yes, she did not take a liking to my Clarissa."

Consuelo hears a trace of sadness in her voice and tries to move the conversation to something else. "I was impressed by the good looking young man who picked up Clarissa last night. I wish I was young; what a catch."

Guadalupe laughs at her indiscretion. "Roberto is like a son to us and is fond of Clarissa. We hope maybe one day he will ask her to marry him."

Consuelo smirks and nods her head in agreement. "He will marry her. That boy is crazy for her."

Clarissa meets the women, unsuspecting of their conversation and discussing the hope of a future marriage to Roberto. She moves closer and embraces her mother and Consuelo. "I hope I have not kept you waiting long." There is much appreciation in these eyes.

It is a new beginning away from the haunting images of El Joven Luis Andres and all that entailed in that house. She quickly departs and kisses her mother and walks out with Consuelo to the road. The road made of dirt and different shape stones, is easier to walk on especially during the rainy season. It is easier for the horses to get by when lugging the carts full of things that ranged from hay to chickens.

Consuelo enjoys chatting away about the mess the guests left behind. She expresses her dislike for Aimee. "La Niña Aimee is a horrible person. She will be the death of me. When she marries El Joven Luis Andres that house is going to hell."

Clarissa listens attentively to her, recalling how exquisite and refined she looked. She was the most beautiful girl she had ever seen. She could not help and think that they would indeed make a lovely couple. It is absurd to think a man like him could have feelings for her. It is ludicrous and foolish to dream that way. Her thoughts go to Juanito, the old man who suffered at the hands of their class; the injustice of being a poor peasant. How could anyone expect kindness from that family? It is a known fact Don Santos is powerful and severe. He is ambitious and does not like anything to interfere with his way of living. It is no surprise he is the most influential man in Guanajuato. She feels compelled to inquire about the old man.

"Consuelo, how is Juanito doing? Is he recovering from his scars?"

Consuelo stops in the middle of the road and stares at nothing ahead. Her mind travels far to search for words. She speaks somberly, "You have seen tragedy already too soon. My mother said to take heed of those who have power. The poor should work for the rich, but from a distance." Consuelo looks at Clarissa intensely. "Do you understand what I am saying child." Clarissa stands quiet, startled by her reaction. Consuelo's demeanor changes and responds sweetly, "He is very lucky and doing better."

Clarissa wanted to press further but Roberto's voice could be heard behind them. They looked back to see him riding toward them in his carriage. His face is handsomely, bronzed by the sun. His joy is obvious at the sight of the woman; his secret yearning for some time. Consuelo enjoys the manner in which he comes alive. He radiates with the strength of a lion and the sweetness of a lamb. It comforts her to know that Clarissa has a man who would care for her. She pushes away the thoughts that invaded her mind for a moment. She is perturbed by the sudden interest of El Joven Luis Andres. It is good she left that place before anything could happen.

"Roberto, you were sent by God to give us a ride into town."

Roberto has a light spirit about him. He has the ability to warm a room with his smile. He is a man with no false pretenses. He is a rare type of man; transparent and genuine. "I came from visiting your home Clarissa. Your mother told me you were on the road to Don Pedro's Bakery."

Consuelo laughs. "You know my cousin Pedrito?"

"He has the best sweet rolls in town."

Consuelo feels comfortable in her forwardness as she moves close to him and touches his arm. "Ay, Roberto if you were not so young I would marry you instantly!"

Clarissa grins at Roberto who quickly blushes in embarrassment. "Let me help you ladies." He moves to help Consuelo up onto the carriage with no problem.

Consuelo is further impressed by the boy's might and ability to make a well-rounded woman feel as light as a leaf. "Clarissa, he will make a wonderful husband."

Clarissa looks at Roberto and feels awkward by her remark. She could feel the warmth of her cheeks rise as Roberto stares at her with a look not like before. She is embarrassed by the insinuation and stays silent. Roberto assists Clarissa as tenderly into the carriage. He touches her with such gentility, fearful of somehow hurting her. Roberto is consumed in happiness at having her near him.

Clarissa, unclear of Roberto's true sentiment is convinced he has only a brotherly love for her.

13

The road gives way to the lovely green pastures as they move toward town. The smell of freshness was all around them, enhanced by the breeze's sweet caress of the many single white flowers. This, coupled by the brilliant green leaves from the trees that canopied the road, made it a pleasure for the senses to enjoy. It is heavenly to see such green, a tranquility of the spirit that is the secret to the strength of surviving the many hardships of life. The Cathedral can be seen as they approach their destination. In the center a lovely gazebo is draped in green leaves, with all the shops (including the bakery) around. The carriage stops in front of Pedro's Bakery. It is a quaint bakery that has a charming vase with fresh flowers to adorn the window as the baked goods are displayed in baskets. Roberto helps the women from the cart as they make their way to the bakery. It is a charming little place. The bake racks are filled with colorful pastries that smell divine. The aroma of cinnamon and vanilla enveloped the palate. The mind gives into the temptation of wanting to consume everything. Consuelo is at home and quickly takes a basket and begins her picking of the sweet delights.

A delightful old man with a contagious smile comes out from the back covered in flour. "Conchita is that you? Where is the girl you have brought me?" He stops and looks at Clarissa with pleasing eyes and gives out an amusing laugh. He is a jovial fellow full of life. "I am Pedro the baker but my friends call me Pedrito. Welcome to your home." He moves to shake her hand and gives her a kiss on the cheek.

Clarissa is at ease, finding him very endearing. She reciprocates a smile and is thankful to know this is her new employer. "I look forward to working hard Don Pedro."

The old man objects. "Don Pedro, nonsense my child, no one in his or her right mind calls me that. I am Pedrito."

She nods her head as she enjoys a sweet roll that bears her name.

Pedrito walks over to hug his beloved cousin whom he loves as a sister. "She is round and sweet like these conchas indeed."

They all laugh as Consuelo pinches Pedrito in the arm. "Good morning Pedrito."

The little old man turns to Roberto and gives him a hearty hug. "Roberto, it is always great to see you my boy." He mockingly measures himself with his hand to see how much he has grown. "Roberto, it seems that every time I see you you're taller."

Consuelo, not being able to resists, adds to the humor. "Pedrito, maybe you're just getting shorter."

What a wonderful environment to be part of, with no false pretensions about them. Clarissa is at ease in this new place and could see only good things awaiting her. The notion that the bread of life was made to enjoy and that sweetness was added by the genuine kindness displayed in this place made it a blessing for her. Although, Consuelo places items on the counter and then expresses her irritation with the guests at the big house; interrupting Clarissa's thoughts.

Pedrito, curious by nature, cannot resist asking of El Joven Luis Andres. "Conchita, has El Joven arrived from abroad? He must be since you're taking his favorite pastries."

Clarissa disposition changes at the mention of the man who left an impression on her. It is absurd that she give him such importance. He is above her station, a man of properties and social importance. She quickly tries to regain her composure without notice. However, Roberto watches how Clarissa's face has changed color at the mention of this stranger's name. His suspicions about last night were left unsettled and now gain rise to speculation. If this stranger had anything to do with the condition in which he found Clarissa, he feels his hand clutch with distress as he stares at Clarissa. She smiles so kindly that his heart forgets his brief fear.

"Clarissa, I will pick you up after work."

She nods her head in acceptance. Consuelo asks Roberto if it would it be too much trouble to drop her off at the big house. He agrees gladly. He is appreciative that she helped Clarissa find new employment away from the big house.

Pedrito wraps the sweet bread in paper to keep it warm.

Roberto moves closer to Clarissa to be near her until it is time to depart.

"Pedrito, please take care of this girl for me. I promised her parents we would look after her," remarks Consuelo as she takes the sweet breads.

He laughs, "Please Conchita, I will look after her."

Roberto looks back one more time before exiting the bakery. His eyes fill with such devotion. The old man smiles at the sweet realization that the young man is in love with Clarissa. The question remains if his affections were reciprocated. It is difficult to tell from Clarissa, who appears guarded with her affections. It is too early to discover her feelings. In time all will reveal itself. She is a lovely child and it is only natural that Roberto would be fond of her.

Clarissa follows Pedrito to the back of the bakery to be introduced to the other baker. A stout woman fights with the dough, making it follow her instructions. Her cheeks are pink and her hair appears black but at the moment is dyed in white flour. Her charm is sweetened by the lack of front teeth. It is probably to the consumption of too much sugar. She leaves the dough and wipes the flour from her and introduces herself. "Bienvenida Clarissa, I am Rosa the bread maker, as you can see. We are happy you will be joining us."

Pedrito nods his head. "Rosa makes the sweetest bread and I am lucky to have her working here." Rosa begins to blush in embarrassment and hits Pedrito gently as to have him stop with the compliments. He gives out a hearty laugh in amusement. "I have to be careful or my arm will be filled with loving bruises." She hits him again. Clarissa finds it engaging, the respect and quiet love they have for each other.

Pedrito provides a brief tour of the bakery and everything that goes into making bread. "It is physically exhausting to make bread, but a great pleasure when your customers enjoy it. Clarissa, you are too charming to be hidden in the back making bread. Instead it will be your job to entice customers to purchase more bread. It is easier to buy bread from a lovely face than an old man." Clarissa, slightly disappointed, was looking forward to learning how to make the different types of sweet rolls. It is as if Pedrito could read her thoughts. "Do not fret. I will eventually teach you the recipes of the various sweet rolls we sell."

Clarissa is shamed by her ungratefulness. It is enough he offered her a job at such short notice. "Pedrito, I am sorry if I appear ungrateful."

He hushes her delicately. "No my child you did not do anything of the sort. It pleases me to know you are excited to learn the craft of making bread," as he laughs.

14

Luis Andres is not as pretentious as his family. He feels comfortable working between the social classes, he thought. As a child he was always intrigued by the life of those who served his family. He would sneak to the kitchen and observe how everyone was natural in his or her person. It was appealing to see a room filled with laughter that was not inhibited by social standard behavior. He liked it especially when Consuelo would seat him and talk to him as she prepared his milk served with his favorite pastry.

He walks through the corridor that leads to the kitchen. He takes the opportunity to be alone while his friends are resting and his mother is entertaining Aimee. The kitchen is strangely empty. He closes his eyes and recalls the horrible event that upset him so much. Why did it bother him so? He hardly knew her to make that kind of impression on him and yet she did. She had somehow succeeded in leaving a mark in his desire for her. She had eyes that captivated his imagination unlike any other woman had done so. He thought of the difference between her and Aimee. It could not be denied that Aimee is a beautiful creature that embodied the desire of any man and more importantly she is of his social pedigree. Yet Clarissa is different in her simplicity. Vanity or greed had not yet corrupted her. He longed to savor the innocence.

His thoughts are interrupted by the abrupt noise of horses coming close to the back door of the kitchen. Luis Andres walks toward the window to see who has arrived. He observes the young man who is helping Consuelo from his cart. He could hear him thanking her for helping Clarissa find a job at the bakery with her cousin. Luis Andres can't help but smirk at the discovery of the girl's new employment. He steps away from the window and heads to the door as to give the impression he just walked in.

Consuelo comes in with a basket of the sweet bread wrapped in paper. She is startled by the presence of Luis Andres in the kitchen. It had been years since he did something like this. Consuelo almost drops the basket on the floor. He moves quickly to help her with the goods. "Joven Luis Andres what a surprise to see you in the kitchen!" She takes the basket and walks to the large table to set the bread in a nice large plate to serve later. Luis Andres laughs. There is a musical richness in the manner in which he laughs. She looks at him and it seems for a moment that she is staring at the little boy from long ago - the one that would sneak into the kitchen and cause havoc among the servants. He was a loving boy and now he was a man. He was less approachable especially the night before. He moves next to her with his charm and inquires about the person who had brought her in the cart.

It now made sense to her.

"Yes, Roberto he is a good boy." She stands quietly arranging the bread while she views his interest in what she is going to say. "He is the young man who picked up Clarissa and took her away from here."

He looked at the tray that is meticulously decorated and takes his favorite pastry. He bites into the sweet roll filled with custard, savoring the creamy filling as she watches him with delight. Luis Andres has magnetism that makes him a dangerous man. He could easily be denied nothing. Consuelo has her suspicions that Luis Andres is curious about Clarissa.

"Is your cousin still making his delicious sweet rolls?"

Consuelo is unaware that Luis Andres is merely confirming his conclusion of where Clarissa was working. She smiles and replies, "Yes, he is still making the sweet rolls you are enjoying just now."

He smiles with a mischievous look behind those large eyes. "When you see him next, send him my greetings." He makes an unexpected move and gives Consuelo a kiss on the cheek like he used to when he got his way as a child.

Consuelo, astounded by his bold affection follows him, speechless with her eyes as he graciously walks away.

They finished early in the bakery. Pedrito did not want to overwhelm Clarissa with too many responsibilities on her first day. It was to be a gradual learning process. She had the rest of the day free to do what she wished until they picked her up.

Clarissa takes the opportunity to ask Pedrito if he would be kind enough to relay a message to Roberto on where to find her. She had a strong desire to go to church and pray.

He nods his head as she waved good-bye. "I will see you early tomorrow."

Clarissa walks toward her spiritual haven. She places her shawl over her head as accustomed when entering the church. She walks passing the Gazebo, unaware that Luis Andres and Jean-Claude wait for her to come out of Pedrito's bakery. Luis Andres persuaded Jean-Claude to follow him on his adventure to seek out Clarissa. His motives are to have a chance to talk to her and get to know her well. Earlier they rode into town; standing out among the town's people. Everyone knew it was Don Santos's son and a friend. The people paid their respect as they nodded their heads in acknowledgement of his family. They paid a young boy to look after their horses while they walked to a small café. Luis Andres wanted to march into the bakery but his friend advised him to wait until an opportune time. Jean-Claude found it peculiar to see his friend react so impetuously. Luis Andres is usually a calm and collected person when it comes to women. There is such urgency in his manner when dealing with this girl. It is a new capricious feeling that will soon expire with boredom, thought Jean-Claude as he observes his friend's anticipation.

They see a lovely figure leave the bakery. This figure has strange effect on them both. He looks to his friend and has him take care of the bill while he follows after her. Clarissa is engrossed in her thoughts and unsuspecting that she is being followed. Clarissa enters the church and pauses with reverence. She heads to the empty pew that faces the front of the crucifix and kneels to pray. Clarissa allows herself to be wrapped in her prayers, forgetting all that is around her. It is in the House of God she feels at peace. There was a time she contemplated the notion of entering the sisterhood. Now her thoughts were of gratefulness and a simple request to erase the feeling troubling her.

"Dear God in Heaven, please remove the image of El Joven Luis Andres from my mind and heart."

There is a sweet beauty in her words as she speaks from her heart. Luis Andres's countenance changes at the pleading prayer of this girl who committed the indiscretion of expressing her feelings. He experiences a sensibility unlike anything before; he is overflowing with warmth, happiness, and bliss. The spiritual atmosphere of the church heightens the seriousness of the emotions discovered.

Meanwhile, Jean-Claude takes a sip of his drink as the leaves from the trees fall on the table outside. He notices a young man walking toward the church. It is Roberto who has come for Clarissa as promised. He strolls to the church with anticipation in his steps. Jean-Claude watches him as he disappears into the church. He decides this would be a fine time to see how his friend is doing. He stands from the table and walks over slowly.

Seeing a young elegant man sitting behind Clarissa surprises Roberto. Roberto's heart feels anguish. He moves briskly toward Clarissa who is quietly praying. It is apparent to Roberto that Luis Andres is taken by Clarissa by the exchange of looks he gives him. He gently touches Clarissa on the shoulder so she is aware of his arrival. "Clarissa, I am here to take you home."

Clarissa gives her last sign of prayer and stands up from the pew. Her shawl drops from her head and lands on her shoulders. Luis Andres moves to help her but is interjected by Roberto who gives him a strong look of dislike. She is in disbelief that Luis Andres is in church. She sweeps into those eyes that succeed in making her heart beat uncontrollably. Luis Andres, on the other hand, is memorizing her lovely expression and the innocent nervousness of being caught. Their eyes lock for a brief moment, suspended in unspoken words. Roberto witnesses the reaction between them, abruptly takes Clarissa by the hand but not before giving Luis Andres a menacing stare.

"Come Clarissa!"

She is shaken by the encounter. How long had he been behind her? Did he hear her confession? She is mortified at the thought of her revelation. Why was he there? What interest could he have with her?

Roberto held her hand, gripping it hard, afraid to let go. He is upset in a manner she had never seen before. There was a fire ignited behind his kind eyes when he saw Luis Andres. He accidentally bumps into Jean-Claude as he flees with Clarissa out of the church. They walk quickly to the cart. He helps her in and does not look at her. Roberto is ashamed and angry he reacted in such a foolish manner. Clarissa worries for Roberto and is upset to see that he is not himself. All her life he protected her and was always generous to her family. He is the brother she always wanted and blessed to have. He is a beautiful person who had some property and enough animals to have a decent living. Yet he gives her family and others much of what he produces. Roberto is a saint.

The road is strangely silent as Roberto and Clarissa drive home. Clarissa's thoughts race - trying to make sense of what just occurred in the church. She is distracted and excited because she had seen Luis Andres again. His haunting eyes revealing tenderness, called her to know him. He is as enticing as the ocean that seductively calls you to deep waters. Roberto struggles with his emotional frustration, drowning his hope of happiness. He fears for Clarissa's heart and impressionist nature. He cannot remove the notion that Luis Andres has other intentions - not honorable for Clarissa.

Jean-Claude walks into the church and sees his friend sitting quietly meditating with his eyes closed. He has a different air about him. "Luis Andres, you look to silly with that grin."

"Clarissa is simply mine."

Jean-Claude responds incredulously, "It seems the young man with her would strongly disagree with you."

Jean-Claude notes Roberto's reaction was not affable. He is going to be a worthy opponent against the interest his friend has on the girl. Luis Andres seems not bothered by Roberto at all. Luis Andres walks ahead of his friend and stands outside the church enjoying the sunshine. He sighs deeply with gratification.

"She makes me happy. I will not let go of this feeling no matter what the consequences bring." Jean-Claude wonders about his friend but stays silent in the matter.

"Let us go home Jean-Claude."

15

Aimee and Doña Santos sit and discuss the intent to solidify the relationship between Luis Andes and Aimee. It is going to be the most impressive event of the season. Aimee is well aware that Doña Santos is strong willed and will make the occasion happen. She is content that Don and Doña Santos took a great liking to her. There are many society girls who could have been considered to marry the most coveted bachelor in Mexico. It is fortunate her family is highly respected with strong financial holdings to make the match possible. Her family's fortune will soon be his upon their betrothal. Aimee is confident that the man she will marry be physically appealing and rich. Luis Andres is undeniably a beautiful man. He is strong with a mysterious air about him that makes him desirable. She accepts the possibility that a man like him would be unfaithful, yet discreet with his extra curricula activities. Alexis informed her of his womanizing while studying abroad. It does not matter to her as long as she holds the title and power behind his throne. Aimee is aware of her beauty and readily uses that to her advantage. She possesses the gift to appear ingénue in the presence of certain men. Her coquettish nature and soft voice can bring any man to his knees when appropriate. It is a known fact that many suitors sought her attention with no avail. She had her heart set on her equal; Luis Andres. She enjoys walking through the gardens on the Santos family property. She contemplates with gratification at knowing she will be mistress of it all. It helps that Doña Santos is becoming increasingly attached to her each day. Doña Santos is preparing everything to announce the formalization of their engagement.

The families previously agreed upon this arrangement. Don Santos is an aggressive man with a difficult disposition. His will is law in the town and Luis Andres demonstrated the same stubborn demeanor as his father. However, Luis Andres had been given many liberties. This will change, it is time for him to settle and take ownership of his family legacy.

Aimee sits near the fountain absorbing the sound of the trickling water when Alexis interrupts her. "How lovely to see you Aimee. You are looking ravishing as always." Alexis sits next to her.

She notices the bruises on his face as he approaches her. "We missed you last night and this morning? I am wondering because of the way you look."

Alexis laughs sarcastically. "I was trying to have a little fun but was abruptly interrupted by my host."

Aimee inquisitiveness caused her eyebrows to arch as she spoke. "Are you saying Luis Andres was the culprit behind your demise? Why would my wonderful Luis Andres stop you from your silliness, unless you were doing something foolish?"

Alexis was enjoying the route to their conversation. "It seems our host has an interest in his hired help and maintaining their honor. I cannot blame him for wanting her for his own. She is quite extraordinary, if I may say so myself."

Aimee's face turns crimson as she tries to regain her composure. She wonders if it is that detestable servant girl Luis Andres showed some attention during dinner. Well, it does not matter anymore. She will no longer be a distraction for her Luis Andres. Alexis observes as her lovely color returns to her face and she smiles. "Alexis, I am surprised. I did not realize you had a palate for hired help. I imagined you to be a man with more discriminating taste," as she looks flirtatiously at him.

Alexis laughs again and replies, "My dearest, I would not have to look any further if you would simply return my attentions."

Aimee is flattered by his constant interest, aware Alexis has always fancied her. He comes from a good family and tried unsuccessfully to convince her to change her heart's interest. It is Luis Andres who is more fascinating ... and simply wealthier. "Alexis, we have gone over this before. I think you are attractive but my heart belongs to Luis Andres."

He laughs yet deep inside he envies his friend. It appears everything he wants Luis Andres has with very little effort. He harbors inside his soul for misfortune to come to Luis Andres as if only to share a little of the frustration of what he feels on wanting something he cannot have. "Aimee you are divinely beautiful yet the peasant girl you scorn seems to have caught not only my interest but Luis Andres'."

She smiles and listens attentively to him.

"As I was trying to introduce myself in a more familiar manner, your beloved Luis Andres came to her rescue and managed to bruise my face, all for her. He definitely has pride of ownership of his property."

Aimee looks away for a moment waiting to remark. "You will be sad to know that Doña Santos removed her from service. It seems that girl left much to be." Aimee waits to see Alexis' reaction but he merely nods his head in acknowledgement. "Alexis, I am quite tired. Why not be a good boy and walk me to the big house."

Alexis happily agrees. He stands and waits for Aimee and offers his hand in assistance. She smiles as she takes a hold of his arm and heads back to the house. Aimee walks looking straight ahead and mentions under her breath, "You will apologize to our host for yesterday's foolishness? It is not worth losing a good friendship for a simple frivolity of ego."

Alexis laughed sarcastically. "I intended to excuse myself for that misunderstanding."

She is content to see that Alexis and Luis Andres would soon reconcile. A small cloud of uneasiness falls over her thoughts about the servant girl who had caused the rift. Aimee decides not to occupy herself with such absurd notions. The important thing is that she is gone.

16

The sitting room is inviting. The warm glow of the fireplace entices those around to sit and enjoy. Luis Andres' painting hangs above the mantel giving the room regal beauty. The painter succeeded in capturing a subtlety behind his look; alluring yet withdrawn. A quiet passion lies behind his eyes, like a jaguar waiting for the perfect moment to unleash its power. Jean-Claude and Luis Andres can be heard as they approach the sitting room. "What are you planning to do with that poor defenseless girl?" inquires Jean-Claude.

Luis Andres moves into the sitting room and heads toward the bar. "How about a drink? Brandy or tequila?"

His friend sits on the sofa near the fireplace admiring the painting. "He did an excellent job making you look more handsome than you are. I think when I go back I will have him immortalize moi."

Luis Andres laughs. "You will never be as handsome as moi, my friend but I am sure he will make you look tolerable," as he pours the brandy into his glass. He brings the drinks over and sets his on the mantel with his back facing the fireplace as he gives Jean-Claude his drink.

"About Clarissa ... well I like her."

His thoughts wander for a moment, entranced by the mere mention of her name. "She is a lovely thing who I must have."

Jean-Claude takes a sip of his drink. "Luis Andres you are being selfish my friend if I may say so myself. You have not given any thought to the girl or her family. How about your family or Aimee? I know your family would strongly disapprove of you fooling around with the poor girl."

Luis Andres sips his drink and sits adjacent to his friend. Jean-Claude is a good friend. They met in school while studying abroad. They have the same notions about the world. Yet Jean-Claude is more idealistic and not quite cynical. He is glad to have him as a trusted friend. Maybe it is the silence of the room and how the flames dance with a hypnotic glow that made him think so deep. Jean-Claude listens attentively to Luis Andres and says nothing.

With determination in his words, "I will wait for her outside of the bakery. I simply need to see her again." He takes another sip of his drink. Alexis, approaching the sitting room, hears a portion of Luis Andres' conversation with Jean-Claude. He realizes Luis Andres knows the girl has been let go. This increasingly peaks his interest. It is information he can use to his advantage. He waits before entering the room inconspicuously.

Jean-Claude looks up from his seat and notices Alexis entering. "Look at what the king of Rome brought in."

Alexis smirks sarcastically. "I suppose I have that coming to me." He walks over to Luis Andres and starts his apology for his behavior. "Luis Andres, it was not my intention to offend you or your staff. I was just blinded with unresolved passion when I saw the girl."

Luis Andres cares little for his attempt at an apology. "I would prefer not to mention that disagreeable moment."

He cringes internally, recalling how he had Clarissa pinned. He must appear unaffected. Alexis behaved no differently than what is expected of his class. He lost his composure only because it was Clarissa. Alexis' actions toward Clarissa were not short of his own behavior. Given the same situation he would have acted the same. His upbringing allotted him that entitlement. Luis Andres enjoys his drink while Alexis recognizes his friends are still upset with him. He will not allow it to spoil his evening and pours himself a drink and joins the men.

Soon after, Doña Santos and Aimee come into the room. Aimee's goal is to look irresistible everyday of her stay with the Santos family. She uses everything in her power to assure the engagement between herself and Luis Andres. Her entrance demands admiration. All the men in the sitting room abide. They stand and offer her a seat. Although Luis Andres is smitten with Clarissa, he yields completely to Aimee in that moment. She is the ideal his family has in mind for him to marry. Aimee is a ravishing creature that belongs to an illustrious rich family. Her education is thorough and appropriate for a woman of her status. She represents the powerful image of the elite in Mexico that is slowly growing to be more like the pretentious Europeans. Luis Andres is clever enough to know that Aimee could be fixated with him and not necessary in love with him. It is the mere vanity of beauty and power that matter. It is the life of leisure with false pretenses that she values. She resembles his mother. It only makes sense his mother would choose someone close to her nature. He knows that like his mother Aimee designs to surrender everything for the ideal of loving someone. His parents managed to live their existence with little affection toward each other. It is a miracle they were able to procreate a child by the manner in which they address each other. They expect their son to continue this apparent legacy. The passion and love are left to quietly harbor in the imagination of their hearts and minds, never to be truly released. He understands his father has been with other women to quench his lust for passion. He is allotted that kind of life as long as it does not disrupt the main household. It is a contemplation to consider for his growing desires.

Luis Andres heads to his mother and gives her kiss on each cheek. "Mother, you are looking lovely as always."

She smiles tenderly, "My darling, I trust that you and your friends are enjoying yourselves."

He is attentive to his mother. "Yes mother. I see that Aimee is keeping you company. May I say she is looking beautiful as always?" Luis Andres warmly kisses Aimee's hand. A fervid sensation travels through her arm by the sweet token. A quick glance of his portrait makes her body flutter with delight. This is the man she wants for her husband. He represents strength and virility as her thoughts transition to all present in the room so graciously.

"Luis Andres you are too charming. Alexis, Jean-Claude, good to see you gentleman this fine evening."

Alexis smiles mischievously as Luis Andres takes her arm and escorts her to the chair; not long before Consuelo comes to announce that dinner is ready. Don Santos and his steward enter behind Consuelo and head to the dinner table. Jean-Claude offers his arm to Doña Santos who gladly walks with him. Consuelo excuses herself and observes Luis Andres' attentions to Aimee.

17

The coziness of the blue room with an inviting view of the gardens below, a round mahogany table piled with imported books and a glass decanter filled with his favorite liquor is a refuge for his thoughts. He gradually opens his eyes and admires his work. He accomplishes to capture her loveliness in his treasured sketchbook. The images seize his imagination and now are found in this priceless book of his. He drops the pencil and caresses his drawing with much affection. Clarissa liberates emotions in him that trouble him and yet he delights at the challenge of seducing her heart and making it his. He is determined to have her somehow; she is the flower in the countryside, often not noticed. It is only God in Heaven that knows of her existence, beauty in simplicity. The corruption of malice and vanity has not spoiled the sweet fragrance of innocence. He would pick this flower for his own admiration. He would surely succeed in having her fall in love with him. Luis Andres already left an impression on the girl by her sweet confessions in the church. He takes a deep breath, closing his eyes briefly, opening them again. He will have to do something about the young man who guarded her so tightly. Luis Andres will keep his relationship secret and afar from those who will not condone it, specifically his family and Aimee. He rests his eyes as he closes the sketchbook and the thoughts of seeing her again.

Luis Andres wakes early to catch the morning bustle of the house. Everyone is asleep. He walks to the stables and finds his father speaking with the steward about business. Don Santos is ordering to have one of the men whipped for negligence with his cattle that had again been separated from the rest of the animals. "These idiots have to learn how to take care of my property. How often must I teach them to be careful? They are worse than the animals. I do not know why I bother. I could have him sent away for my consistent loss in his mistakes."

The steward does not want to carry more responsibilities than he has to. "Don Santos, Juanito is not as young but he is a good worker. He found the animal and it did not stray far."

Don Santos does not approve of his steward interfering in his decisions. He believes he is a just and noble Patron and resents his insolence. "I do not need you to call for his defense! I am a generous man. Let him choose, he can either be sent away or receive a proper beating for his lack of responsibility. That is final."

Luis Andres listens to his father. He is repulsed by the nature in which he deals with the workers. It is understandable that the town fears him. It is respect that stems from fear. His father has power and he knows how to execute it when things need to be done. Luis Andres hopes not to be noticed as he walks quietly back to the house with no avail. "Luis Andres, come here." He has no choice but to comply. "This indeed is a surprise to find you awake early. I am glad to know you're not lazy like many of the young men of today."

Luis Andres stands quietly and smiles. He is anxious to depart from his presence. "Father, I am going into town to get reacquainted with this land. It has been awhile and I think it is best to do so."

Don Santos stares at his son with interest. Well my boy I think it is a good thing. It is important that they begin to see you through these parts. Luis Andres, it will be your obligation to keep our name strong in this land."

It is difficult to oppose his father. His future is being decided for him whether he wants it or not. The freedom he feels is less real. Now he is obligated to continue the inheritance for his family. This is the burden of being the Santos family's only son. He knows the next order of business is the discussion of his future marriage to a suitable young lady.

"Luis Andres, it is time for your engagement to Aimee. Your mother and I want to set a formal date. Son, you understand we have been waiting for this moment for a long time. Aimee is a beautiful woman that comes from a prominent family in Mexico. I know you do not have any inconvenience to formalizing this arrangement." Don Santos' voice changes to a more serious and stern tone. "I know you are not completely opposed to the idea of having Aimee as your wife. You will make me proud when this blessed event takes place."

Luis Andres listens attentively to his father's expectations. Don Santos has a manner of imposing his will on his son. He was strict and at times cruel to him as a child. He demanded he always be strong and not display any weakness. "The revelation of weakness leads to a man's downfall," is what he preached to him. His childhood memories resurface when his father scolds him harshly. As a child Luis Andres escaped into the garden to hide behind the trees and cried. In time he learned to bury his hurt and anger.

"It is settled Luis Andres. I will have your mother begin the arrangements for the engagement festivities."

Luis Andres' fate was sealed.

"Father, I will now take a ride into town. We can discuss the particulars later." He excuses himself and heads to his horse to have it saddled to go. Don Santos, satisfied with his arrangement, leaves the stable with his steward.

Luis Andres' horse mesmerizes him with the rhythm as the buff hits the earth. The path into town is inviting with trees that shower the ground with leaves and wild flowers that weave into the grass paving the way. It stimulates the senses as the tranquil sounds and beauties envelop him. This place has an abundance of natural charm that allows for reflection. Luis Andres ponders on his means to gain Clarissa's confidence. He would have to approach her carefully, with good intentions.

He is conflicted by his capricious desire for both women. Clarissa
especially, with a depth to her simplicity that he yearns for despite
knowing that she would never be allowed in his social circle. It is a
troublesome situation yet he will find a way to reconcile it. He ties the
horse near the bakery and waits for the proper moment to meet with her.

18

Roberto drops Clarissa off at the bakery. He informs her he will be late picking her up. She smiles and agrees to wait for him in the church. He is not happy with this idea. He is bothered by the encounter between Luis Andres and Clarissa. Roberto fears they will somehow meet again. "Clarissa, I would feel better if you stay with Pedrito in the bakery."

She embraces his arm tenderly to assure him not to be afraid. "Roberto, I will be alright. You know how important it is for me to be in church with my Virgin looking over me."

Roberto looks into her eyes that sweep his soul away. He nods in retreat and steps into the carriage with a smile and goes. Luis Andres witnesses their interaction and is overcome with jealousy. He feels a sting of anger rise. He does not enjoy seeing Clarissa be affectionate towards another man, especially Roberto. It is clear to him that Clarissa must be his. He waits a little longer before entering the bakery.

Clarissa places the fresh bread out as the door opens. She doesn't look to see who enters but welcomes them to the bakery. "Bienvenido to the bakery. We have fresh bre…"

She becomes aware of the tall figure of an elegant man smiling at her. It is Luis Andres standing before her. Her breath feels light at his sudden appearance in the bakery. He walks slowly toward her with his eyes, fixed on her. She feels the sudden blush go to her cheeks and looks down to regain some composure.

"Hola. How are you? I came to see how you are doing this fine day? I was worried."

Clarissa is taken back by his remark. Why would a man of his caliber be interested in a simple person like her?

He sees she is questioning his intentions. "You are probably wondering why I am here. The truth is that you have left an impression on me."

Clarissa looks up with mixed feelings and remarks, "You are generous with your kindness but there is no need to worry about me."

Luis Andres moves toward the bread to ease her anxiety. "Clarissa, I have the best intentions for you. I want us to be friends. I want to know you better. I promise to keep my distance."

She feels her head swirl. Her feet struggle to keep their balance. He notices and moves to help her from falling. Clarissa falls into his arms. Luis Andres holds her gently as she looks into his eyes; filled with such emotion and warmth that it permeates her being. Clarissa experiences a security in his strength. "I will not hurt you," whispers Luis Andres softly.

Pedrito walks in humming a song and notices them together. Clarissa is embarrassed by his misconstrued perception. Luis Andres helps Clarissa and walks over to the old man with his charming charisma.

"It has been a long time since I walked into this bakery."

The old man grins in his youthful spirit. "You rascal, you were just a boy and my cousin had you by the hand as you tried to sample all the sweet rolls."

He gives out a boyish laugh that makes Clarissa smile. He seems real and common with no falsehood about him. She wonders if her inhibition could be exaggerated by the fear of knowing who he was and what he represented.

"I could not help it. You have the sweetest rolls in the world," as he quickly steals a glimpse in her direction.

Clarissa looks down to regain her self-control from his subtle stares.

Pedrito is content to see the boy as he prepares a basket for delivery. "It is good to see you again Luis Andres, you rascal. This lovely girl will help you with your purchases," suggesting in his coxing manner. "Well excuse my abrupt departure but business is business." The old man takes the basket and heads to the door departing with a smile.

Luis Andres keeps the door open until Pedrito is off. Clarissa goes behind the counter to provide a barrier between them. He walks to the counter with his eyes fixed on her. There is a light that resonates from his eyes and smile. He is eloquence embodied in a splendid being. Clarissa can easily lose herself in this whirlwind of emotions.

He sees Clarissa's hand on the counter and softly picks it up and bestows a gentle kiss. His lips are soft and warm. She stares down at her hand, shocked by his action. He stands up abruptly, surprised by his forwardness.

"Clarissa I apologize. I do not know what came over me. I must confess; I am captivated by you." He looks into her eyes. Luis Andres sees her with sincere vulnerability. The energy between them is magnetic. "May I visit you again? Anywhere you want. I am at your disposition."

The manner in which he pleads makes it difficult for her to resist his request. She allows her heart to dictate her will. She nods shyly and softly says, "Yes."

19

Luis Andres is overwhelmed with happiness. "Thank you. You make me very happy. Where can we meet today?"

Clarissa, astonished by everything that is happening, could only think of Church. "You can meet me at church after work for a moment. It is my favorite place to go."

He imagines her as an angel from heaven. "I will leave you to your work. I will see you then in church." He bows his head and departs but not before giving her a wink.

Clarissa allows herself the joy in the insanity of her bubbling feelings.

The light scent of myrrh infiltrates through the church. It is peaceful with only the quiet meditation of a few parishioners occupied in prayer. Flowers adorn the sacred institution while white candles softly illuminate the alter. Luis Andres sits in the last pew near the door. He is not a particularly religious person. He is excited about having the opportunity to be alone with her. He does not know what to expect from his first meeting with her.

The nature of their first meeting takes a spiritual turn he did not expect. As he stands in the church, surrounded by spiritual ornate objects, Luis Andres feels conscious of his intentions with Clarissa. He feels the religious statues stare at him with reservation. As he contemplates waiting, a lovely vision appears in the entrance of the church. The light from the sky beams from the ceiling and illuminates her face. Clarissa is unaware of how divine she looks.

Clarissa is nervous as she walks into the church. Her heart runs ahead hoping to see him. Her mind is struggling to make sense of it all. It is a great risk to meet a man against her better judgment. Consuelo and Roberto advised her to stay away from Luis Andres; yet she could not resist the temptation to see him again. She longs to look into those eyes, if only for one last time. The church is a haven for her. It is her favorite sanctuary. This place offers comfort against the cruelty and shortcomings life presents. Clarissa steps inside the church and finds Luis Andres sitting in the pew near the door. He is handsome with a smile that brightens any darkness or sadness she may have felt. Clarissa moves quickly before Luis Andres has a chance to greet her. She bids her respect in prayer before sitting in the pew ahead of him, away from his look. This is the second time they are together in the church. The energy between them is increasing, as the silence seems inevitable.

Clarissa's nervousness amuses Luis Andres as he waits. He finds her irresistible. He loves how her shawl drapes her beautiful head and how stubborn strands of hairs escape from the covering. While he observes, Clarissa quietly tries to regain her breath that escapes her.

Luis Andres moves closer, "Thank you for coming. It means more than you can ever imagine. I was beginning to fear that you would not come."

Clarissa softly responds, "I keep my promises." Although her mind tries to escape her existing reality, she finds the courage to ask him what she wants from her." "Joven Luis Andres, I do not understand the reason for this meeting." She asks him while looking at the crucifix that stands above the altar.

Luis Andres moves closer to her ears, "Clarissa," He pauses before continuing, "You make my heart happy." Clarissa's body shivers with delight as he continues speaking. "I know you cannot believe me. However, I stand here in church to tell you my heart is filled with joy when I see you and all my thoughts are about you ever since I laid eyes on you." He stands and walks to the pew, where she sits and sits next to her. The sensations of the world fades away; they hear, feel, see only each other.

Luis Andres takes her small hand in his. She glances into his penetrating eyes that yearn with emotion. Her heart leaps with rapture, permitting her to be taken away by this dream. "Clarissa, I would never hurt you. How can I make you see you are the most important person in my life?"

Her eyes began to water at his declaration. Her mind wants to reconcile but the truth of their social difference floods around her. "Joven, please, even if what you say is true I must remind you I am poor. Your family would never permit us to see each other. We are very different. The only interest men in your position want with a girl of my station is ..."

Luis Andres would not allow her to finish her remark. "Clarissa, my intentions are honest and furthermore I love you!" His words escaped so naturally. They were meant for her to hear. "I do not want you to worry about my family or friends. I will take care of it." He could witness the vulnerability of her soul through her eyes. His heart overflows with euphoria.

Clarissa's heart is his. Tears stream from her eyes.

"How am I going to tell Roberto and my family about you?"

His hand caresses away the tears from her face. "I will care for you and your family. I must ask you to trust me on this matter. Our families will have to accept our love. However, until then we must be careful and protect this relationship. You must not tell anyone until the proper time."

Clarissa tries to maintain her composure. Her life is marvelous to be blessed with the love of the man of her dreams. She could not fathom in the farthest depth of her mind that he would be expressing his feelings for her in church. It is beautiful.

"Clarissa, please call me Luis Andres. I want to know you have accepted my love."

She releases a sweet smile. "Luis Andres, Roberto will be coming soon to pick me up. I would not like him to see us together."

He nods his head and kisses her hand again. "I will come to visit you soon my querida Clarissa." He stands up and walks away contently.

Meanwhile, she kneels down and prays with joy over her new found happiness.

20

White clouds hang in the blue sky; a lovely day made more beautiful by Clarissa's presence. They stroll through the little plaza like they do every Sunday after church. Guadalupe and Jacinto go home to prepare a humble meal, while Roberto and Clarissa enjoy their walk. She is somehow different. Her eyes reflect the brilliancy of stars. The air about her is light and confident. He has known her all her life and yet a mystery lies behind her now. He is ashamed to know that a monster grows in him. He loves her devotedly and cannot perceive sharing his life with any other women. The horrible sensations of anxiety, anger and sadness now plague him. The thought of her with someone else mortifies him. He is conflicted in the desire of wanting only the best and the rage of her affections belonging to someone else. The incident with Luis Andres in the church haunts his mind profusely. The chemistry between them both is evident and disturbing to observe. He cannot erase the way they looked into each other's eyes. He covets that moment and longs to capture the magic exchanged by them. It is a nightmare that nudges quietly behind his reason. Roberto counteracts this fear with the knowledge that she is away from that man. There is no possibility of engaging in each other's presence without knowing first.

He has spoken to her parents about his intentions to marry Clarissa soon. It is his greatest wish to share a life together, providing her a better life. He will do everything in his will to make her love him. He knows that at the moment she holds him in a special place for a brother or good friend. It is not this position he hopes in time he will change this. Roberto finds it entertaining to see her laughing for no apparent reason. The light breeze dances in her hair as they walk around the gazebo of the central plaza.

"Clarissa, what makes you laugh?"

"Robertito," Clarissa lowers her head in embarrassment of being surprised by his awareness of her silliness.

"What?" he urged. "I would love to know?" Roberto is waiting for her response.

"It is just a feeling that comes over me. It is hard to explain."

He looks at her intensely, trying to decipher what hides behind her words. Clarissa looks away from his intense scrutiny. She cares for Roberto dearly and is now aware he has special feeling for her; feelings she cannot reciprocate. The irony is that before setting eyes on Luis Andres she had hoped to marry Roberto. She is comfortable around him. He offers security and honesty. He is clear like water that moves by the mountains. You can set your feet with no fear of surprises. It is easier to choose a life with a man like Roberto, yet it is too late for her. The problem now lies within her heart. The core of her existence now completely belonged outside her social status, with the simple ability to hurt her. The feelings that emerge within her are a delirium unforeseen. Luis Andres had proven to be a gentleman; behaving properly around her with courteous attentions. He declared his love and devotion to her. Clarissa's heart swells with unreserved adoration every time the memory of his look and his words about their life together. These captured moments of the past make her laugh spontaneously. She wants to share this with the world. The deception lies in the promise she made to not tell anyone. It is difficult to keep these thoughts from all those she loves, especially Roberto, whom she admires.

Clarissa affectionately hits his arm and changes the subject. "Robertito, we should head to the house. Consuelo will be coming to the house to join us for dinner."

He nods his head in agreement and playfully remarks, "I take it that you will not answer my question." He smiles and adds, "Maybe certain things are best kept secret in a woman's heart."

Clarissa looks down, slightly bothered by his remark. She laughs and proceeds to put her arm around him. "Robertito, you know I care for you." He smiles sweetly at her and basks himself in the moment, enjoying their walk together in silence.

Consuelo walks into the humble home bringing sweet bread from her cousin's bakery. It is nice to be relieved from the demands of Doña Santos, especially with the recent engagement announcement. It will be the official wedding engagement party for Luis Andres and La Niña Aimee. Her morning was going well until she uncovered disturbing news that Luis Andres was a frequent visitor to the bakery. This troubled and vexed her because of the dangerous implications to Clarissa's family. If Doña Santos found out, she would dismiss Guadalupe and Jacinto from her services. Consuelo does not want to mention anything to Guadalupe until she speaks to Clarissa. She fears for the young girl's fate because of how charming the boy can be. It became obvious to her that he was interested in Clarissa from the moment he fixed his eyes on her. She had hoped that the distance between them would protect her from his intentions but it appears otherwise.

Guadalupe is making tortillas; the dough dances and swirls in her hands. Beans are simmering in the homemade stove her husband comprised from stones outside. The table is set outside to enjoy the beauty of the warm evening. The chicken Roberto brought is roasting under the flames. He also brought coffee to enjoy. It is times like these among friends and family that are too far and few. The only sad drawback is that Don Santos' steward called Jacinto back to work.

"Consuelo, I am glad you are able join us for supper. Come and sit next to me while I finish the tortillas."

Consuelo looks for Clarissa. "Guadalupe, where is Clarissa?"

Guadalupe places the warm tortillas in a cloth to keep the heat and sustain the warmth for dinner. "Clarissa is with Roberto. They should be coming home soon." Consuelo releases a sigh of relief. Guadalupe looks at her with concern. "Are you feeling well Consuelo? Let me prepare you tea."

Consuelo moves to help her with the tortillas. "Do not fret over this old woman. I am fine and happy to hear that Clarissa is with Roberto. He is a nice boy and they look good together."

Guadalupe smiles. "Yes, he is like a son to us."

Consuelo continues with her thoughts of Roberto. "He would make a good husband for Clarissa. I wish he would take the initiative to ask the girl!"

Guadalupe laughs. "All in good time, we cannot press matters of the heart. Roberto will ask her when she is ready."

In a tone of concern, "Do you think Clarissa will accept him?"

Guadalupe knows what Consuelo is doing. "Why would she not accept him? Do you suspect something I don't know about my daughter?"

"Of course not, it was just nonsense on my part."

Guadalupe places the tortillas in a basket. "Consuelo, I know my daughter loves Roberto. She has a light about her when she goes to work every morning now. It is Roberto who takes her to work every morning. It has bloomed so recently but love is like that. It heeds no warning."

Consuelo exclaimed, "Guadalupe, the boy is in love with your daughter."

Guadalupe turns to Consuelo. "I know he is in love with Clarissa."

Consuelo's eyes widened with delight. "Jacinto and you consent?"

Guadalupe flips the last tortilla in her hand. "Yes. Clarissa is fortunate to have a man like Roberto to love and care for her. We could not have asked for a better blessing."

Consuelo is put at ease by the course of events. Roberto would now be guarding her against misfortune. She is excited by this news. "Has Clarissa accepted?"

Guadalupe stacks the tortillas inside the cloth. "She is not yet aware. Roberto is waiting for the proper time."

Consuelo nods her head, hoping her words are true. Somehow she senses it is not the case.

Roberto and Clarissa approach the house and see that everything is set for supper. Consuelo is outside with Guadalupe enjoying the warmth of dusk. She notices her father is not home and realizes he was called to work. She walks toward the women. "Consuelo, it is good to see you," as she gives her a kiss and tender hug.

Roberto takes his hat off and extends his hand to Consuelo. "Buenas tardes Consuelo."

She moves toward him and gives him a hearty embrace, disregarding the formality. "Come here boy, give me a proper hug."

Clarissa finds the situation humorous and cannot contain her laughter. "Mama, where is father?" as she bends to kiss her on the cheek.

"Don Santos called your father to work. It seems they need more help to set up for the big engagement party."

Consuelo is agitated. "You would think they could spare him on a Sunday, to enjoy with his family."

"We cannot afford that kind of luxury. Sadly we are at the mercy of their generosity". Guadalupe states this as she takes the pot from the fire and places it on the wooden table.

Clarissa moves to help her mother. She is curious by her mother's mention of an engagement at the big house. She inquires unobtrusively, "What kind of engagement is happening at the big house of the Patrones?"

Consuelo blurts out. "El Joven Luis Andres and La Niña Aimee are going to be married!"

Everyone was surprise by the matter of Consuelo's exclamation of the news.

Guadalupe with more serenity informed her daughter. "The engagement is to formalize the relationship and union of the new couple."

Clarissa felt a strong force strike her stomach, taking her breath and causing her to almost lose her balance and drop the pot of coffee. Roberto swiftly rushes to assist Clarissa. It astonishes everyone present.

Alarmed by her daughter's reaction, "Clarissa, are you alright my dear?"

Her face flushes and her heart races like mad. She forces herself to appear composed. "I am sorry mama. I must have slipped on something on the ground." She places the pot safely on the table.

"Mija, you could have been burned. The pot is very hot. It is good Roberto was here to help you."

"Thank you Roberto," as Clarissa tries to regain her composure. Her heart aches and wants to release the anguish within. Her eyes struggle not to water. She quickly wipes them. Everyone knows something is not well. Consuelo and Roberto's suspicions are confirmed.

Guadalupe is in the dark, unaware of the true sadness her daughter is experiencing. "What is wrong Clarissa?"

Consuelo feels guilty for blurting the news. She is saddened by the realization of her fear for Clarissa. She has fallen for El Joven Luis Andres and her demeanor reveals the true nature of her sentiment for him. Clarissa looks at Roberto who is staring at her with sorrow and compassion. Consuelo attempts to make light of the situation. "Guadalupe, I am sure it is nothing. It is probably the scare of dropping the hot pot that has her like this. As you said she could have burned herself severely."

Guadalupe, not quite convinced, thinks it best to change the subject. "Let us enjoy the meal."

Clarissa turns to her mother. "I am sorry to frighten you mama."

Guadalupe, disquieted by what she sees in her daughter's eyes, embraces her child. She discerns something is happening to her. She would have to wait until her daughter is ready to relate whatever is troubling her. "My dear child, you know I am here if you need anything."

Clarissa closes her eyes and embraces her very lovingly. The tender moment shared between them makes Consuelo and Roberto's hearts feel moved.

Consuelo shakes her tears, "Enough! My food will soon taste like salt. Let us eat for I am hungry."

Roberto smiling, "Yes, let us enjoy this fine supper."

Clarissa releases her mother. They sit around the table while Roberto offers a prayer for the meal to be blessed. Clarissa sits next to Roberto and begins to serve him. Consuelo contemplates what a lovely pair they make. This is how it is supposed to be; Roberto and Clarissa. She looks into his eyes that are filled with so much adoration. He knows her plight. How long has he known? She wonders as she places his plate down. It does not matter now. She was a fool to believe that he would leave everything for her. Luis Andres lied to her in a terrible manner and she simply fell for his lie. The loss of this romantic dream is such disappointment.

They lit the candles as the darkness began to roll in. The kettle made of adobe simmers the aromatic coffee. Its vapors rise into the air smelling wonderfully sweet, as it makes its way to the senses. The shadow of a man approaches. Clarissa's father Jacinto arrives, tired from the demands of his job. Guadalupe quickly prepares his plate. He is happy to see everyone who means something to him present on such a lovely evening.

Clarissa hugs and kisses her father. "I am glad you are home."

His face is aged by hard labor and sun exposure. He takes his hat off and places it on the table. "I am glad to be home my child."

"How was your day Jacinto?"

He takes a sip of coffee before responding. "Plenty of work to be done for the festivity, it seems that the Patrones' son is finally getting married. The engagement is going to be the biggest thing we have seen in these parts for a while. He wants us early to finish up with any last minute things. My dear, we may have to stay the night depending on what they need."

Clarissa is overwhelmed with sadness; she cannot hold back the tears any longer. She excuses herself and runs out quickly. Her actions leave everyone speechless. Roberto follows her. She stops by some trees at the end of the road. She is crying uncontrollably. The pain is deep and she does not know what to do to relieve the deception inside. Roberto observes the moonbeams caressing her hair. He walks to her and softly speaks.

"Clarissa, you cry for Luis Andres."

21

Her pain is an abyss that descends and steals her happiness away. He holds her close. She trembles in his arms. Roberto wants to remove her suffering. Her words drown in her tears as she speaks, "He said he loved me and we would be together." She continues to sob, "He lied, Roberto, he lied, and you warned me."

Roberto is angered by his deception but is sensitive to Clarissa in the moment of anguish she is experiencing. "I am sorry Clarissa. He is typical of his class. He just wanted to play with you." He feels his heart beating as he caresses her hair. "I know you are hurting Clarissa but you must forget him." His thoughts rage with anger. Luis Andres came close to deceiving her. He fears what his true intentions are with his Clarissa.

She holds on to his shirt. "Roberto, forgive me for causing you grief."

Roberto is jealous at how completely she gave her heart to that man. Yet he holds her in his arms to cry under the tree branches that shade them from the moon and stars above. The night breeze sweeps through the branches and the soothing sound calms the rhythm of Clarissa's breath. Roberto waits for the moment to confess his feelings and intentions to marry her. He had hoped to ask her under different circumstances. Clarissa gradually releases herself from Roberto. She was appreciative that he was helping her deal with her pain. She is almost loose from Roberto but he continues to hold her hands. His eyes unlock the emotions in his heart.

"Clarissa, I love you."

She tries to prevent him from uttering such words but with no avail. He continues with soft words. "I was shattered when I suspected there was a possibility of another." He pauses for a moment, "I know you do not love me like him but I can give you a life of honesty. My feelings for you have always been honorable. You are the only woman I could see spending the rest of my life with."

Clarissa's sadness grows at his revelation. "Roberto, I care for you but I love Luis Andres. It would not be fair to you."

Roberto moves closer to her space, "Clarissa, I know you have feelings for him yet you have said that you care for me also. I can make you happy."

She sees a mirror of her own pain in his eyes. He loves her sincerely and her family adores him like a son. Although her heart is burdened with the love for another, her mind is clear on the truth. Luis Andres is a misguided illusion and Roberto loves her unconditionally. He holds her in his arms again.

"Clarissa, would you be my wife. I will sell everything and we will move to a different town, away from this place. We will start anew; you and your family together." He closes his eyes imagining this future together.

Clarissa allows herself to believe in this new life with Roberto. She sees no alternative to her sad predicament. Clarissa responds in a soft whisper, "I will be your wife." He holds her tight, afraid of ever losing her to anyone.

Clarissa pushes her pain down and accepts her destiny with Roberto. She will be happy with him. Teardrops fall from her eyes, staining her cheeks.

22

The house is luminous with flowers and candles throughout. The festivities for the engagement party are in full bloom. The tents have been placed in the gardens. It is to be a spectacular party. Musicians and entertainers arrive for the night's performance. Luis Andres, the most sought after bachelor, is finally settling down with the loveliest socialite of Mexico. The Santos and De La Madrid family will soon unite their power and fortune with the matrimony of their children. It is a dream come to pass for them. Doña Santos and Aimee finalize the arrangements for the wedding. It is decided that the wedding will occur in the Cathedral outside the hacienda. Doña Santos has formalized the date with the priest; within the next six months. Aimee convinces Doña Santos to push the wedding date closer. She has suspicions best to entangle him while she has the ability. The engagement will solidify his commitment to her.

Luis Andres and Jean-Claude walk through the house, noticing every servant busy at work, ensuring everything is perfect for the evening. Guadalupe and Consuelo pass by, setting flowers in the parlor. He looks at Clarissa's mother and feels a pang in his heart. This is the woman who had been blessed to conceive Clarissa and bring her forth to this world for him. Guadalupe is a goodhearted creature, always reserved and keeps to herself, invincible at times. She takes care of each assigned task required with diligence. Consuelo is more spirited. She is jovial and kind. He stares at both women and greets them as they pass by.

"Buenos Dias."

Guadalupe nods respectfully, "Buenos Dias Joven."

Consuelo does not respond. She ignores him and continues walking. This is unexpected for both men.

Jean-Claude finds Consuelo's behavior humorous and releases a laugh. "Luis Andres, what did you do to the poor woman that put you in her bad graces?"

He is surprised by her blatant display of dislike. "I do not know but it seems she wants to kill me with her looks."

"Keep away from her," Jean-Claude sarcastically added.

"I think I will take your advice, or at least until the fumes are gone."

They walk outside to enjoy the day. It is unbelievable to see the commotion over a formal engagement. Jean-Claude is in disbelief over the preparations for the event. Luis Andres seems irritated by it all. He is indifferent to the matter. His reflections seem to slip away to a distant place.

Jean-Claude interrupts him, "Luis Andres, tell me how it feels to go through this marriage when it is obvious that your heart belongs to someone else?"

He looks at the vast commotion before him and then responds, "I do not think about it my friend."

Jean-Claude does not believe him and presses further. "You think about a simple girl who believes in all you say."

His comments sting. "She has a special place in my heart and I will care for her always." His words are earnest.

At that moment Don Santos approaches them as he remarks, "All this is just an agreement that must be made among families."

Jean-Claude adds, "Families with fortunes to be made?"

"Yes," Luis Andres retorts dryly.

Don Santos appears greater than most of the men around him. He is proud of the arrangement of the union between his son and Aimee. Luis Andres feels frustration with the man he knows as his father. His life has been decided for him from the moment he was born. He resents this most of all. Don Santos always imposes his will and influence on all his actions. The only thing he feels are his own are the feelings he harbors for Clarissa. He discovers heaven in her beauty and unselfish love he will not share with anyone. He will protect this lovely secret from anything that may spoil it.

Don Santos takes a box from his jacket. He looks down at it with tenderness and strokes it. It is unusual to see him display any kind of emotion. He is by nature austere and direct. He hands it to Luis Andres and explains the significance of the item contained in the box. "My son, this was given to me by my mother. It is a necklace that has been passed down from generation to generation. It is intended for the woman who will be sharing your life forever."

Luis Andres takes the box and opens it. He finds a brilliant necklace, like stars on a blue night. He closes it quickly and places it in his pocket. He smiles and replies. "Thank you father. I promise it will be worn only by the woman who inspires life into my soul."

Don Santos nods and excuses himself. "Excellent! I must depart and get ready to greet our guests."

Jean-Claude waits for Don Santos to depart before making an inquiry about whom the necklace will be worn by. "Aimee is going to wear that beautifully."

Luis Andres smirks, "I'm not intending it for Aimee. This belongs to Clarissa."

He is astounded by his friend's decision and pats him on the back in agreement. A servant approaches Luis Andres.

"Joven Luis Andres, there is a man asking to speak with you. He is waiting outside by the doors." His eyebrows curl up in wonderment. The servant informs him he had asked specifically for him regarding a serious matter and would not disclose his name. Curious, Luis Andres and Jean-Claude walk to the door to see who wishes to speak with him. As they advance to the doors, Luis Andres sees the man anxious to speak with him is none other than Roberto. This is unexpected as they diplomatically proceed to him.

"Buenos Dias." Luis Andres sees the contempt in his face. Roberto reserves his anger as he speaks. "I am sorry to bother you on this special day for you and your future bride." He continues speaking, staring coldly at the man he despises. "I want you to leave Clarissa alone. She is going to be my wife. I expect you to respect this."

Luis Andres feels his anger rise yet keeps his cool countenance and responds. "I was not aware you were engaged to Clarissa?"

Roberto does not appreciate his tone. "She accepted yesterday. She knows about your true intentions with her." Roberto's voice trembles with emotions as he continues, "How could you deceive her like that, breaking her heart the way you did, making her believe you loved her when you are marrying another? I will not let you hurt her again." Roberto walks away, not waiting for a response by Luis Andres.

Jean-Claude notices his friend clutch his hands in anger. Luis Andres says nothing but follows him with his eyes as he disappears. He feels a heaviness fall over his soul; Clarissa knows about the engagement. It now makes sense why Consuelo was upset with him. The part that bothers him is Clarissa marrying Roberto. He feels sick to his stomach at the idea of another man having her. He will not allow it. He calculates what to do. Although he desires to resolve this now, he will seek her out tomorrow as intended.

Jean-Claude is aware the news of Clarissa's future marriage to that young man stirs something in his friend. Luis Andres is engrossed in his thoughts. It is destiny that moved in to set things straight. Luis Andres is to marry Aimee and now Clarissa has accepted Roberto. It is better this way, especially for Clarissa. He knows Luis Andres will not be able to defy his family and marry her. "Luis Andres, it is better this way. It is obvious he loves her."

Luis Andres walks away from Jean-Claude, heading back to the house and says nothing.

Jean-Claude stands quietly alone, looking toward the house. A moment later he feels a premonition that something is not well.

23

The evening is welcoming all the guests to the anticipated party. The Santos family stand and greet their guests as they walk to the garden where the tents are set out. The ambiance is filled with colors and music that resonates through the house. Aimee took extra efforts to look stunning. She is the envy of all the women present for marrying the man they all desire. She stands statuesque, with an air of meticulous elegance. Luis Andres is handsome with his bewitching eyes. They are an ideal couple, a well-made match. The families are satisfied with the arrangements. The night is filled with congratulations for the families. Luis-Andres is withdrawn; yet attentive to Aimee. Alexis teased her earlier about her fiancée's preference for the hired help. She dismisses anything negative that might infringe on her present state of happiness. It does not matter that Luis Andres is entertaining thoughts of servants. Aimee is going to be Mrs. Santos, his wife.

Jean-Claude is seated next to Alexis, who is flirting with the young ladies, occasionally stealing a glimpse of Aimee who looks ravishing. Earlier he met with her in the veranda having coffee. They were alone relishing the morning sunshine as they suddenly observed Luis Andres and Jean-Claude walking toward the front of the house, disappearing from their sight. Alexis is frustrated that Aimee would not humor him. She is contemplating her life to be, in this house. It makes her grin with delight to realize she has the support of the family. Alexis moves in closer to admire Aimee's beauty. Although she finds him irresistible, at times her thoughts center on her life to be, in this house as the wife of Luis Andres Santos. It makes her smile with delight to know she has everything prepared for the big day. Alexis finds her simply desirable, despite the knowledge he can never have her. He envies Luis Andres in the most torrid manner; yet he must be diplomatic to enjoy the social connections he offers. The sun makes her soft hair shimmer like precious gems. His thought is to touch to her softness, to weave his fingers among the strands of gold. He observes her lips as she sips her coffee. He has an overwhelming sensation to taste the forbidden fruit of his desire. He is not able to resist the temptation and he spontaneously steals a kiss.

She does not anticipate the boldness of his desire and yields for a moment. They are not aware Consuelo had quickly walked in and out, witnessing everything. Aimee pushes him back in anger, realizing she is jeopardizing her future.

Alexis laughs. "It is good to know you do not find me completely revolting."

Aimee takes a sip of her coffee trying to remove his taste, "Do not flatter yourself." She is upset with him. "How impertinent of you, we could have been seen you idiot."

He enjoys her fury. "Do not concern yourself Aimee. I can only be grateful for the lovely gift." She looks at him and smiles sarcastically. Alexis returns the smile and exits. He is satisfied with the stolen kiss as well as her response.

The highlight of the evening comes with the sound of clinking glasses. Don Santos stands up to toast his son and his beautiful wife-to-be. There is ambition projected in his voice as he speaks about this proud moment. He captures the attention of his guests with his commanding presence. The similarities between father and son are physically obvious. They both have an intriguing aura about them and are mesmerizing. Those present feel Don Santos' speech as they toast the couple. Aimee enjoys the evening next to Luis Andres. She holds his arm tightly being the envy of all there. He looks at her with more than civility; imagining it is a million times Clarissa. He looks around the room as they hold their glasses high and toast the occasion. The wedding will take place in six months time, a decision his parents decided without his consent. Luis Andres smiles graciously as their social world swirls around them with congratulations. The sounds of the orchestra begin to wind through the gardens. Everyone enjoys the hospitality of the Santos family. Even the most particular guests give the highest praise. The newly engaged couple graces the dance floor. They are a lovely sight moving so eloquently. The dance steps they take heighten the beauty of the music. They are a charming duet and appeared to be the perfect pair.

The morning is lost in a blur of images of last night's soiree. The families are satisfied with the outcome of the evening. Luis Andres on the other hand, is troubled by the thought of losing Clarissa. His fear saturates his dreams of seeing her evaporate into nothingness. He wakes to a sweat of anxiety and desire. He is not able to deny himself the burning desire of wanting only her. He struggles with his conviction concerning Clarissa. It is absurd they should be separated because of her misfortune of being poor. He knows deep inside it is not right that economic inequality should be a factor against them. He could do the honorable thing and release Clarissa. Or, go against the tide and marry her and start a life together away from the convention of his society. He is educated and could be free from his obligations to follow the traditional path of power expected of him. Luis Andres could pave a new adventurous life made of his own conviction. It is a chance to create a new world for him and Clarissa, yet bitterness rages within his own passions. He is inconvenienced by Clarissa's faith and his intentions to protect and respect her always. How was he to reconcile his thoughts to benefit his situation? Luis Andres could not lose Clarissa. She is everything that makes him happy. Her blooming sweet spirit and the melodic sound of her voice makes the song of any bird pale in comparison. His thoughts turn briefly to Aimee. She is exquisite who stands cold like a Botecelli's Venus. Aimee is a product of her surroundings. Luis Andres will plead his love until Clarissa consents to have him. He closes his eyes; shuts out the blue night and welcomes the blank darkness.

Clarissa walks to church after a long day at work. She is tired of the sorrow that fills her heart. The light is dim in her soul as she fights to regain some insight from the painful lesson of love. She carries the weight of loving him despite his cruelty and insincerity. Clarissa hopes to forget him in time with the help of Roberto. It is only fair to love him with the same devotion she loves Luis Andres. These are idle tears for a man unworthy of her love as she feels the emotions rise again to her throat. The wetness from the tears leaves traces of pain on her cheeks.

She unexpectedly feels someone take hold of her hand with gentle force preventing her from moving toward the church. Luis Andres pulls her into himself; embracing her. A wave of emotions floods her soul. His fragrance is a blend of freshness that intoxicates her mind. She wants to be in his arms forever. What a wonderful way to depart this earth; with his warmth and strength enveloping her. Yet it could not be; anger quickly reminds her of his deceit. Clarissa pushes herself away from him with hot tears streaming down her face. She has an anger he has never seen before, a reproach that will sting his memory.

"Do not touch me! I know about your wedding to her," as the tears continue to flow.

Luis Andres feels flattered by her display of jealousy. He smiles slightly at knowing she loves him with such conviction. He moves closer and speaks softly, "Clarissa, listen to what I am about to tell you. You should never doubt my feelings for you."

She nods her head vehemently, "You lie! I was just a past time; a moment of fun."

Luis Andres grabs both her hands; they are eye to eye as she tries fighting him with no success. "Clarissa, you are the only woman for me. It is you whom I love and no other. If I told my parents about us they would separate us. Think of your parents ... they would suffer the repercussion of my family's prejudice."

It is true, Don Santos is not a kind man and Doña Santos dislikes her. She looks into those eyes that offer soothing comfort to her anguish. He embraces her with quiet affection she does not resist. "Luis Andres, thank you for your words but it is obvious we are not meant to be together." She looks down as she brokenly says ... "I have accepted Roberto."

"You cannot marry him. You are mine. I am the only one who could love you. Clarissa we are going to be together. I have something I want to give you." He takes the box from his vest and gives it to Clarissa. She opens it and is blinded by the shimmer of it; a necklace made for a princess. He continues to speak, "This has been in my family for a long time. It is intended for the bride." Clarissa looks at him with confusion. "Yes, I want you to be my bride Clarissa. I will arrange for us to be married in three days."

The fruit of her love is sweet again hearing the dream lyrics reciting from his lips. "Please Luis Andres do not play with my feelings. It will surely destroy me."

He tenderly kisses the lips he coveted for so long, the sweetness flavored with salty tears. Her soul takes flight to the world made for him and her alone. The wedding is to be held in the garden outside the plaza. Clarissa is sad to hear it will not be held in her church. She offers to speak with the priest but Luis Andres feels it could harm their chances of getting married if it leaked out to his family. The Santos family is a great supporter of the Church and vested interest could find it beneficial to disclose such information. The only person invited as a witness is Jean-Claude, who supports his endeavors. She wants her family to be present as well as Roberto. Her Roberto, who was like an older brother, will be disappointed by the news. It will be painful but he will come to accept Luis Andres. He will realize how he wronged his character. This is how she rationalizes her thoughts about his plight. They walk to the gazebo near the church and sit by a bench that hides them from sight. He holds her hand as he speaks about the preparations. She looks to the Heavens ever so grateful of her newfound bliss.

"Clarissa you cannot tell anyone until we are married ... not even your parents. I will get word to them as soon as we are settled in our new home. Our families will have to accept our relationship."

She will soon be his wife. Clarissa can no longer doubt Luis Andres' love for her anymore. She allows her imagination to capture their devotion and have it imprint itself in time. The melodic birds perched on the trees pay witness and immortalize their love in a song. They sit under the trees making plans for their new life.

He holds her hand tenderly enjoying her company and the happiness it brings him. He kisses her causing the blush to rise to her cheeks. "My beloved Clarissa, I wait for our day together. We will make a new life based on love and love alone; away from all the nonsense and frivolity. We will be happy even if my family does not accept our arrangement."

Clarissa stares at him ecstatic about living a life with the man who owns her heart.

After some time Luis Andres departs, satisfied with his encounter with Clarissa. He finds it difficult to leave his beloved. He eases her mind with promises that all things will resolve themselves accordingly. Clarissa's body is light with delight. She floats high above relishing the celestial blue sky and soft white clouds.

It is surreal knowing her dreams and reality merge to create this wonderful euphoria.

24

The warm breeze is inviting to the perfect stillness of the day. Roberto meets Clarissa, finding her deep in her thought, sitting on the bench. Engrossed in her own happiness, she is not aware of Roberto's presence. He is happy to find her inner strength renewed. She enjoys her surroundings. He waits for her to descend from that glorious place that mesmerized her.

"Clarissa."

She turns and smiles at Roberto with such a lovely glow about her. His heart melts in disbelief at the sight of her countenance. There is a hope behind those eyes that had shed tears of despair not long ago. His spirit leaps at the miracle of seeing her this way. Clarissa takes his arm and they head home. They embrace affectionately, walking to the beat of cobblestones beneath their feet. They stop at the cart and Clarissa feels the urge to embrace him again. She feels his heart race beneath his shirt. He welcomes this unexpected gesture, but the manner in which she holds him is strange; as if she is trying to say so much but is not able to. The moment is perfect. He holds her in his arms. Clarissa never thought this could happen to her. How can she expect Roberto to understand her situation? She loves him so differently. What she would give to have it be different. Clarissa was moved to say anything, anything to the man who had been so wonderful to her and her family

"Roberto, my life has been blessed. I will never be able to repay you for your consistent kindness and unconditional support." Emotion floods her eyes.

He feels the wetness of her tears on him. He raises her chin gently revealing her lovely face that displays mixed emotions. "You have done more than enough for me Clarissa and have made me happy." He kisses her on the forehead despite his longing to kiss her on the lips. He helps her into the cart.

Pained with her conflictions, she utters softly, "Roberto you are truly a saint."

"No, I am just a man in love." She stays silent, meditating on all that has been said and done.

In a few days she will be Luis Andres' wife and not Roberto's. Her life will be dedicated solely to living and loving him. She hopes Roberto has it in his heart to forgive her. Clarissa does not doubt his great compassion. She must believe he will understand her decision. Before he departs Clarissa quickly embraces Roberto unlike anything he felt before filled with so much affection. Clarissa wanted to leave Roberto with the understanding she truly cares for him. He is significant in her life. She tenderly whispers she cares for him always and kisses him on the cheek. The moment is the sweetest of his life. He enjoys Clarissa's elusive affection. She waits for his departure before entering her home.

Strangely quiet, only the sound of the blue night is heard. Her parents had not yet returned from work. It is a late night for them. Today brought plenty of unexpected surprises. She reminisces about Luis Andres as she lights the candles located in the room. Her heart hurts with unbeknownst happiness. Sweet sensations run through her blood, exciting the soul. Luis Andres makes her feel this way. The uncertainty scares her yet she yields whole heatedly because it is he. She looks at the portrait of the Virgin, whom she thanks with silent tears. Tears mingled with bliss and pains, the cause of her abrupt departure. Heaviness fills her heart with the sadness of leaving her parents with the news of her elopement and Roberto's heartbreak.

Clarissa cannot deny her heart, feeding on the promises of devoted love and happiness with Luis Andres. He will sacrifice his way of living to start a family with her. He is asking her to do the same, but only briefly, until the storm of the news of their marriage becomes acceptable. She finds it difficult to think that Doña Santos will ever accept her. From the moment she met Doña Santos, Clarissa felt her grave disapproval. She wonders about Aimee and her reaction? It will be awhile before his family accepts her. Her family is different. They are gentle, humble folks. They may have reservations, but will come to accept him. She is sad no one she knows will be at her wedding. Her tears came rolling down.

Guadalupe walks in to see her daughter crying devotedly to the Virgin. "Clarissa?" She says softly, "What is wrong?"

"I was just thanking the Virgin for everything in my life." Her mother holds her in her arms. Clarissa cries uncontrollably. "I love you and Papa so much."

Guadalupe caresses her daughter's hair. "Hush, I know you do. We love you so much too." Guadalupe looks to the portrait of the Virgin.

25

The three days pass quickly. Luis Andres secretly makes preparations for the anticipated night. Jean-Claude is vital for the success of his endeavor. He prepares everything for the simple but lovely ceremony. He wants Clarissa to feel special, always. He purchased a lovely home secluded from everything that could invade their privacy. It is a piece of heaven, high up in the hills with a view of the trees and fields around them. It is a lush landscape with the smell of fresh spring blooms. A breathtaking paradise for lovers. The perfect hideaway. He arranged for provisions to be delivered daily. Clarissa will never have to go into town. All that remains is to excuse himself from his family temporarily without raising suspicion. He has calculated everything to assure the day will be perfect. He is excited the day has finally arrived when he will have her to himself. Luis Andres and Jean Claude are ready to depart on their escapade but not before seeking his mother. He spoke to his father earlier to inform him about his departure. Don Santos is fine with his decision to take care of things. He feels a trip to Mexico City will do his son good. A little pleasure before settling down is always good for men, thought his father.

He finds his mother and Aimee together, making wedding preparations. Luis Andres and John-Claude bow their heads in respect and give them a respectable kiss. Aimee is happy to see her fiancé before his departure. She had been informed he is going to the city to get her something special for the wedding. He will be gone for a few weeks. She is at ease to know

Jean-Claude is accompanying him. Doña Santos looks at him with reservation. It is such a spontaneous trip that gives her little time to think about what she might be forgetting to have them pick up in the city.

"You have a safe trip my son. I will miss you terribly, but I am glad to have Aimee to comfort me."

Aimee reciprocates her smile of appreciation.

Luis Andres is civil and understands his mother's tactics. "Mother, it pains me greater to depart from you and Aimee. However, the sacrifice must be made temporarily for the sake of the wedding. I want my bride to have a lovely wedding that she will never forget."

Jean-Claude finds the narration a bit much.

Aimee blushes in delight. "I am indeed the most fortunate woman to have a wonderful fiancé who is so attentive."

Luis Andres smiles and kisses her hand tenderly before departing.

"I will keep you in my thoughts for a speedy return," remarks Aimee sweetly.

26

Clarissa wakes before the sun's early rise. She prepares coffee for her parents who are waking to another day of hard work. She brings it over to her father who gives her a sweet kiss on the cheek. "Muchas gracias my dear girl," as he sips from his clay mug.

She goes to the room where Guadalupe opens her eyes to the aroma of the sweet brew. Clarissa sits next to her, giving her a tender kiss. "Good morning mama."

Guadalupe takes the clay mug from her hands. She closes her eyes and inhales the warmth the coffee offers. It is enough to wake her for the start of a new day. Clarissa's heart is heavy knowing today will be the last day she will spend time with her beloved parents. Guadalupe stares at Clarissa and sees something is bothering her. Guadalupe places the mug down and embraces her child, fearing something is not well. It is a sensation that tugs at her heart. Yet time is impatient and Doña Santos will not wait. Guadalupe gently sweeps away the hair from her face and tells her how much she loves her. Clarissa smiles and nods her head in acknowledgement. In a moment's time her parents are off to work and the house is empty.

She walks through the house for the last time. She takes her most valuable possession; the rosary her mother and father gave her as a child. Made of simple beads, the gift is precious nonetheless. In front of the picture of the Virgin she asks her in prayer to keep her parents and Roberto safe while she is gone. Her tears flow quickly as she wipes them away. Roberto will pick her up today. He cannot see her like this. She hears him coming and quickly takes the letter she has written, and with a kiss, places it on the bed as she rushes out of the house.

The morning sunlight streams into the bakery through the window. Pedrito is occupied making deliveries. He notices Clarissa is unusually distracted. "Niña, in what cloud are you riding?"

Embarrassed, she pauses for a moment, "Sorry, I was just thinking nonsense. I will have to depart early today."

The old man smiles, "Do not concern yourself, Roberto will be alright."

Clarissa pulls out a letter and hands it to Pedro. "Don Pedrito, can you please give Roberto this letter. I forgot to give it to him this morning. I will be indebted to you."

Very curious thinks the old man, that she hands him a sealed letter. "I think he would prefer if it came from you directly."

Clarissa is lost for words. She feels ashamed and looks down almost releasing the pain she feels.

Don Pedrito does not insist and lightly accepts it. "Do not worry. I will make sure he gets the letter."

She nods in appreciation.

Clarissa leaves the bakery ready to meet her future. It is a beautiful day, as the sun will soon give way to the blue night. Her heart is full of anticipation. She moves slowly as in a dream. The church comes into focus and there by the steps Luis Andres stands waiting. He waits with something in his hands. He looks handsome with his dark hair and lovely eyes that call her to him, a celestial vision incarnated in blood and bones. He moves toward her and hands her the box. "I hope you like the wedding dress."

She looks at him tenderly. Clarissa cannot imagine that her presence makes him genuinely feel better about everything in the world. He takes her arm and leads her away. The sky and stars play homage to their distinctive moment. The blue night is beautiful as they stand in the garden in full bloom. He wants their love to be consecrated by all of nature. The moon conspires to make their dream come true. She comes into view like an angel descending to earth. The simplicity of the white dress adorned by a white rebozo takes his breath away. Jean-Claude was taken by the same vision. Clarissa is simply lovely. She moves to the sweet breeze that accompanies the night. All are transfixed by the vision of pure innocence and loveliness.

Clarissa does not recognize the priest or the other gentleman in the ceremony, except for Jean-Claude. She feels a nostalgic pain for those loved ones missing from her wedding. Luis Andres places the necklace upon her neck. The stars envy the brilliancy of those stones, which embody his commitment to her. A towering sensation takes over her body as a teardrop rolls down her cheek. Luis Andres kisses it away and she smiles. They clasp hands as the ritual begins. They recite vows of eternal love in the natural sanctuary made of creation. Jean-Claude stands silent observing his friend's happiness with Clarissa. The true testament of their relationship will soon be tested.

The emotional rapture of the ceremony intertwines Luis Andres and Clarissa.

"Clarissa you make me complete."

The words echo in her ears and are made sweeter when he seals their love in a passionate kiss. She feels his strength as he embraces her. He draws her soul to his lips. Clarissa surrenders her love to him in the kiss. Those who pay witness cannot deny the affection between them. The young priest quickly steals a glimpse at Clarissa and then looks away. He congratulates the couple wishing them all the happiness. Jean-Claude gives Clarissa a sweet kiss of affection and embraces Luis Andres before they depart in the carriage he leased for them.

Clarissa places the rosary in Luis Andres' palm. "This I give to you is very special, simply it is my life. It is all that is dear to me. What you hold in your hand has given me strength in times of hardship and pain, even the pain of almost losing you. I want you to now have it as a wedding gift. All my love is yours, Luis Andres. I will be always with you in spite of everything. This rosary will be my heart that you hold and will protect and keep you."

Luis Andres is touched. He will treasure this for the remainder of his life. He kisses the rosary and holds it close to his heart. Clarissa is kindled by his gesture as they board the carriage. He holds her in his arms while she closes her eyes in happiness. The world seems to move quickly around them. Love is a web of intense feelings that is encapsulated in these beaming souls. They now journey to their ethereal heaven prepared only for them.

Their home is a colloquial sanctuary canopied by trees. Stars adorn the sky as she stretches her arms toward the heavens. Luis Andres looks at her with the fire of desire. His eyes invite her to swim among the storm that lies within him. The passion that grows in her brightens as they enter their home. The house is fragrant with white flowers. Luis Andres heads to the bedroom. Clarissa hides her face in his chest to hide her embarrassment. He feels her trembling in his arms. He will have to be careful and gentle with his delicate flower. He gently places her down on the bed; beautifully dressed in white flower petals. Candles illuminate the room creating a dreamlike atmosphere. Clarissa's heart leaps with a warmth that kindles her soul. It is a light flame that gradually grows with the desire of her heart. Her body trembles as fear suddenly emerges. Luis Andres senses her anxiety. He holds her in his arms and strokes her hair, wanting her to be at ease. He looks into those eyes of wonder. She is innocent and naïve. He will lead her.

"Do not fear me Clarissa. I will care for you gently."

Clarissa loves him completely. She closes her eyes and abandons herself, entrusting him. Clarissa loses herself swimming in the storm of his soul. She releases herself in his kisses relinquishing her passion within. All that stands is swept away. They move to the rhythm of their hearts; two bodies splendorous in unison, igniting the dark night.

Morning comes as they lie together in their new life. The magic of their first night is unlike anything ever experienced. Her scent is imprinted into his soul forever; the beauty of unexplored innocence as he navigated over uncharted passions. These experiences now belong to him. He contemplates her in sleep as she molds into his space. A thousand beams of light permeate from his soul. Luis Andres has found the meaning of life through Clarissa. She taps into the reserved part of his being locked from everyone including himself. He holds her in his arms, in the heaven they both created. He closes his eyes and allows his spirit to soar among the clouds in the sky with his angel right beside him.

Jean-Claude waits at the inn not far from where Luis Andres and Clarissa now live. He is uneasy with everything that has occurred. A heavy shadow veils the wisdom he once thought he had. His friendship with Luis Andres is important to him. Jean-Claude does not always agree with the tactics and manners in which his friend handles situations. He waits patiently for his guest. He has something special to give him for a job well executed. The ceremony was beautifully crafted and the performance was better than expected. Jean-Claude stands up and greets a gentleman, the individual who was commissioned to create an illusion of sanctity. Jean-Claude hands him a small parcel of money.

The gentleman takes the money and sarcastically remarks to Jean-Claude, "Thank you so much for the generosity."

Jean-Claude responds sternly, "This matter is to be kept confidential."

He stares at Jean-Claude intensely and nods his head. As he walks to the door he looks at Jean-Claude, "I will remember how memorable it was to play the part of Judas Iscariot. The betrayal of someone you trust for a bag of silver coins; it is priceless. How simple the ability to deceive that who you love most. What a tragedy."

He exhales disappointment filled with laughter. "I have to say this was my best performance but not my proudest."

As he walked away, Jean-Claude crashed into his seat and asked for a drink.

27

Roberto stood in front of Clarissa's house waiting. The heaviness of the night was unbearably thick. His hands were trembling as a drop of anguish stained the letter that Don Pedrito had given him. His greatest fear had come to pass. Clarissa left with him. Luis Andres had managed to persuade her to go with him. It was not fair to love someone entirely only to have them love someone else. The world seemed to cave into the darkness of his sorrow. The cold air moved into the empty space of his heart that belongs to her. He loved her and nothing could change that. He lamented not being able to save her. Clarissa's fate was sealed to suffer. Luis Andres was the bastard who would steal her innocence and discard her in time. How would he save her now and recompense for his damage to her? Her affliction would be great. He hated Luis Andres for the cruelty of his deception to this sweet girl. Roberto cried with the dark night and his anguish as company. He was nothing without Clarissa. She was lost to them. The only resolution was to move as quickly as possible. The discovery of the unexpected shame would be great an embarrassment for them to handle. Clarissa was their only child and her fate now lay in the hands of El Joven Luis Andres

Guadalupe's sorrow was difficult to bear. It was hard to accept that her child had been misled by none other than Luis Andres. She hoped that Luis Andres would be kind and caring with her daughter as Clarissa's letter had proclaimed. It was a mystery how all this came about. All this time it was Roberto whom they suspected she loved ... never El Joven Luis Andres. They were left with many unanswered questions. Guadalupe looked at Consuelo, who knew more of Luis Andres than anybody else in the room did. Consuelo brought her a cup of chamomile tea to ease her sadness. Consuelo was aware that Luis Andres was interested in Clarissa but never imagined that he would fabricate such an intricate scheme to take her away. Consuelo did not doubt that they boy had feelings for her. She believed strangely that he did love her, enough to infuriate his parents if they found out. He demonstrated a keen interest in her from the moment he saw her. His eyes came to life at the mere mention of her name. Yes, he loved her in his own way.

"Luis Andres is different from his parents. I know that he would not intentionally hurt Clarissa. I believe he cares for the girl ... no he loves her."

This remark surprised and angered Roberto. "If he loved her as you say then he would not have ripped her from the arms of those who love and care for her. Foolish Clarissa, what have you done?"

Consuelo felt for Roberto, who was consumed with rage at losing the women he loved. It was hard to swallow. Guadalupe continued to sob quietly. Roberto was determined to find Clarissa and save her from the clutches of Luis Andres no matter the consequences. He would take her even if Luis Andres had his way with her. It was not her fault that she was young and impressionable.

Consuelo was uneasy about them leaving so soon. However, it would have to be in the evening as not to raise any suspicion about their abrupt departure. It also meant that Consuelo would not see Guadalupe anytime soon; or ever again. It was unfair but understandable. They would have to start their lives elsewhere. They agreed to leave as soon as it was plausible. They got their belongings in order before leaving. Roberto was not obligated to go with them yet they were appreciative that he did. He was their son despite the circumstances behind their daughter's fate. It was a trial brought about by life to test their endurance and faith. It was the only way they could reason with all this.

Roberto could not define how long they would be gone but he prepared for a long trip. Consuelo discovered that Luis Andres and his friend were running errands in Mexico City for the wedding. They would head out to the city to find them. Consuelo had to come to terms with losing a good friend. She cried for the vacancy left by their parting after becoming accustomed to the routine of working together. They said their farewell and shared the sorrow offered by the dusk of the day. Roberto lead the pilgrimage on his horse while they followed in his cart filled with the little memories they could take with them. The wind blew a slight adieu and Consuelo felt asunder by a frightening premonition she had not the strength to stop them from what awaited them.

They traveled on the long and dark road for days. They stopped alongside for provisions and to inquire if they had seen the couple in search. The pendulum of time seemed to be ticking against finding Clarissa, they thought secretly. They wandered like nomads driven by the wind to find some trace of hope. The kaleidoscope of beauty found in nature could not be enjoyed. It was definitely shadowed by the absence of her. Their spirits were heavy with the burden of incertitude for the future. It was black clouds that brought heavy rains that suddenly consumed the clear sky. They stopped to take a break from the showers pouring from above as they sought shelter in a near town. They had little appetite but enjoyed a simple hot meal. Guadalupe had come to terms with the possibility that she might never see her daughter. Her hopes rested that Clarissa was happy and well. Roberto was attentive ensuring that everything was comfortable for them. He was a constant assurance that things would be better despite believing in his heart otherwise. He looked exhausted yet smiled warmly. They were his only family that he loved and respected. Roberto took the burden of all cost even though they opposed.

Guadalupe went to Roberto and embraced him tenderly such that he could not resist and buried his heart into her rebozo. "Roberto my son, you have been such a blessing to us. We could not have asked for a better son. I know this load is hard to carry yet you continue with our family. I can only pray that you could find some peace in your life. You deserve more than the love of my daughter. She will one day discover the truth."

Jacinto bowed his head in silence. It was an awkward position to be placed in. As a man he was indebted to his continued kindness. His devotion to his lost daughter was unparalleled. He was aware that another man in his place would have never forgiven and accepted Clarissa after volunteering to go with another man. He was a man for a greater calling; a man who would do well in the cloak of a saint.

The rain subsided and Roberto was reluctant to continue on the road in the present conditions. He felt it best to wait until tomorrow to proceed and to stay at a local inn. Guadalupe and Jacinto would not hear of it. Jacinto patted Roberto on the back and escorted him outside to get ready to depart. "Roberto, I think it is best to move on. You have been more than generous with us. We can rest closer to our destination."

The fresh raindrops perpetuated the scent of green nature to release its perfume. It was soothing to travel with the light of the evening peeking out from the clouds. The music of the night increased as they journeyed through the small road of the mountain. It was important to take it slow because of the sharp curve of the hill. The drop below was steep and spiraled to the green abyss. The night was cold as Roberto moved ahead with the horse. The ground was wet and rocky, making the cart struggle upward.

The moon and stars began to dim into the vast night; instantaneously the rain began to fall hard. The bolt of thunder erupted from the sky tracing its mark. The horses, confused by the commotion, rushed onward recklessly. The fervor of the lighting struck the ground near the cart. This caused the animal to move insanely; thrusting itself and the cart along with Guadalupe and Jacinto over the cliff's edge. The abhorrent cry from Guadalupe's voice resonated beyond the clashing of the storm.

Struck with terror, Roberto stood petrified as the cart quickly disappeared into the dark grave below. The rain poured mercilessly on him as he stood in the sudden silence of the evening.

28

In the comfort of their bed Luis Andres stirred by Clarissa's weeps that
invaded her sleep. He moved her gently, concerned by the agony she was
experiencing. Clarissa cried in terror as she sprung from the dim slumber.
He held her close to himself assuring her it was only a dream. She was
like a small child in him arms disturbed by fear. "Clarissa my love, it was
only a nightmare. I am here with you."

She whimpered inconsolably, "It was horrible," as she drowned her voice
into his chest.

He did not like seeing her bothered by a mere dream. "My darling, tell me
what the dream was about that has frightened you." Luis Andres was
tender as he caressed her hair. He had a wonderful way of alleviating any
anxiety in her. His voice was pleasant yet had so much strength. He was
her champion that could make any insecurity disappear. She was
overflowing with relief that she sometimes feared it would all disappear.
This however was horribly different. The nature of her dream was
unsettling. It birthed a sudden small vacuum in her heart for her beloved
parents.

"Luis Andres, it was my parents. It was dreadful. I saw a black crow that
led me to a church. A funeral procession was going on. I was inclined to

give my respects. The sorrow was great and my heart palpitated as I approached the front. I could not make out who was the priest. I continued to walk slowly toward the pulpit. The wailing became louder and the facade of the crucifix seemed to weep real tears. I stood waiting to give my respects. The person before me cleared and my eyes were fixed upon the bowed head of the serving priest. When he looked up I realized it was Roberto and my eyes quickly dropped only to find myself staring at my beloved parents whose soft faces appeared to be in an eternal sleep." Her voice choked with sudden tears unable to clearly sound the words.

Luis Andres kissed away the tears and comforted his beloved. He explained to her that it was because she missed them greatly. He promised her that soon they would be reunited again. He caressed her face trying to remove that sadness that now revealed itself.

The bold gesture of spring to bloom its ever-alluring fragrance made it difficult to depart. He had been so blessed with the prosperity of love. Their time together seemed so short. All the countless days and nights together in this paradise seemed to consolidate into one lovely memory. Luis Andres was sad by the famine he would soon feel away from her. The absence of her countenance would serve to haunt him every day. The sketches he had drawn of her would be a small consolation to the real thing while parted from Clarissa. The dynamic passion of their love was now his light. She was a visual pleasure of delight with those dancing eyes that moved to him. Clarissa had attributed beyond beauty that merit recognition and appreciation. She loved unconditionally in spite of her shortcomings. She was grateful for everything bestowed on her. She was clear like the water not yet stained by meanness and falsehood. She was the light that unraveled his heart to loving her only. Luis Andres was changed. This whirlwind of romantic emotions capitalizes every single second that passed them. He adored her and was troubled by the rare nightmares that would sometimes steal her sleep. It was on those occasions that she seemed vulnerable to sorrow. He wanted always to be there, to comfort her and to restore her smile.

Luis Andres could not stay longer as he exhausted all his time with Clarissa. He did not anticipate staying this long. The time had arrived to face the other truth that stood between his happiness. Jean-Claude had been a loyal friend taking care of all his errands to the big house. Now it was his turn to be separated from her breath and warm blood for a few months. They stood watching the view of the green before them with the flowers swaying to the rhythm of the soft breeze. It was a pleasant quietness found in the sound of water trickling down through the stones. The day was resplendent. Luis Andres held her hand as they took pleasure from their time together. They had discussed the importance of him going back and settling his affairs with the families. He explained that he would be gone for a few months but would always send word to her with Jean-Claude.

It was painful to be departed from the man she loved the most; she understood her plight. He had sacrificed so much for her that it was the least she could do for him. Her days had been bounteous with bliss. Clarissa had shared many pinnacle moments and facets of his devotion and kindness toward her. Luis Andres could be reserved and mysterious when found alone with his thoughts. It was these times that she wondered what convictions stirred his thoughts. Clarissa felt it best to leave him alone with them. He had given her a glorious paradise marked with the colors of his affections. "Luis Andres, I will remember you as we are now. How does one thank the stars for the life you have given me? A celestial angel incarnated in blood and bones. You are my true gift; the sweet truth that opens my heart. Although we may be separated forever I can be glad of leaving this earth knowing you love me."

Luis Andres could say nothing. Clarissa managed to move inside that dreaded discovery. He took her in his arms, clutching to her body. He wanted things to stay as they were. He closed his eyes; shutting the despair that was swelling within him.

29

The sweet echo of her voice rang in his ears as he traveled the journey back home with his friend. Luis Andres was constantly swimming in thoughts about how to make the best of his situation. He dreaded having to face the inevitable challenges that awaited him. His long absence gave way to critical speculation by his mother and Aimee. His father merely dismissed the whole thing as his son's departure of old passions before starting his respectable family with Aimee. Jean-Claude had been evasive when discussing his friend's whereabouts and doings. He was efficient with all his responsibilities required for the anticipated wedding celebration.

Aimee internally struggled with the fire of anger over Luis Andres' long absence. She was uneasy by the possibilities that some wild woman bewitched him and held him prisoner. However, there was the remote thought that would slip in on rare occasions … mostly when provoked by Alexis that he fled with Clarissa. It did not help the matter by the sudden exodus of her family. Don and Doña Santos were upset by the inconvenience brought about by Guadalupe and Jacinto's disappearance. They cursed them more out of anger and frustration than anything. It would be difficult to imagine the sad misfortune that followed them soon after leaving their home. They had been loyal hard working people that said very little. Doña Santos had entrusted her with certain duties that required experience and training. It was a great nuisance she could not forgive. Guadalupe and Jacinto would never be welcomed in the town without some negative retribution. The dissident taste left by their abrupt departure was permanent. The Patrones were inflexible in their compassion or lack of. The task fell now on poor Consuelo to assist Doña Santos with things.

Luis Andres and Jean-Claude came into view of the Hacienda. The day's light was eclipsed by the evening. He found himself estranged from this place that was his home. Luis Andres had been gone longer while residing in Europe for years, yet this time it was different for him. He longed to be in the arms of Clarissa and the place he had created for them. Jean-Claude took notice of his friend's gradual transformation. He was a changed man; a better man for knowing her. "Luis Andres don't look so down. We are here; remember your family and Aimee are anxious to see you again. They did not appreciate moi coming alone without you. At least look like you miss them."

Luis Andres smiled at his Jean-Claude, "I cannot thank you enough my friend."

They both walked into the house not before instructing the help outside to assist with the items purchased. They could hear voices from the sitting room where the family was gathered. The lights flickered brightly as they enjoyed conversing about the upcoming wedding. There was an unpleasant weight in his stomach hearing about the quick approaching date with his bride to be.

The sight of her precious son elated Doña Santos. She dropped everything to embrace and kiss her boy. Aimee gave debut to some tears in his anticipated return. "Luis Andres it is good to have you back. I have missed you," as she stood.

He embraced his mother tenderly and kissed her. He walked to his fiancée and civilly kissed her cheek. Don Santos and Alexis observed his indifferent manner with Aimee. This struck a bad chord with his father. Luis Andres greeted Don Santos and Alexis formerly as well. Jean-Claude got comfortable and poured a drink while Luis Andres sat between Doña Santos and Aimee de la Madrid.

"Luis Andres, you had me worried. I was beginning to think I would never see my son again. What in the world would keep you out there so long? Poor Aimee was very worried."

Luis Andres smiled at Aimee as he went to hold her hand, "It was extremely difficult to be parted from you."

His father interjected, "Leave the boy alone. The important thing is that he is home and all will resume as planned, right my boy?"

Jean-Claude watched how the slight resentment crept into Luis Andres' voice. "I would have it no other way father," as he stared at him. The energy between them was thick. It was clear who the veteran was in this situation. Don Santos was not convinced about his son's sincerity. He would make sure that everything would be in proper perspective for him. Aimee held his hand warmly. Alexis watched closely at her attempt to warm up to him. It was apparent that Luis Andres was being diplomatic with her. It was sadly humorous, her vain effort to get his attention. It bothered Alexis that Aimee was more concerned with affirming her engagement. He stood silently observing their interaction.

"My dear Aimee, my apologies for causing such concern. There really was no reason to worry. I was taking care of things that are important."

Jean-Claude smiled by the double sordid remark.

Aimee was content to have him near her. "Although I should be very angry with you, all is forgiven." She spoke sweetly as she caressed his hand.

Doña Santos was relieved and happy to see thing were proceeding according to her plan.

Aimee took the moment to dangle her bracelet. "Luis Andres I almost forgot to thank you for the gift you sent with Jean-Claude. It was sweet of you to buy this bracelet for my wrist. Although I would have preferred that you would have given it to me personally."

He was surprised by this first news of the gift and a gives a quick look to Jean-Claude, who shrugged his shoulders. "I am glad to see that you are enjoying it." He moves to kiss her hand tenderly as she blushes. "Please excuse me. I am feeling somewhat fatigued and think it best to rest after a long and fastidious trip." He released Aimee's hand not before giving it another kiss. He turned to his mother and bids good night. He stood and looked around the room, excused himself and walked out.

He walks into his room, heading to the window and opening it. His restless spirit welcomed the sweet breeze. He touched the breast of his jacket as he looked into the garden outside the window. He took the rosary given to him and gently kisses it. Luis Andres had an overwhelming desire to be reminded of her. He pulled out from his pocket the sketchbook with her face. He stood contemplating her sketch with her face, frozen in the moment. It was phenomenal the inability to control emotions that seem to take over one's sanity. Luis Andres was so distracted by the image of Clarissa that he was unaware of his father. Don Santos had entered his chamber. He observed him steadily with interest. Luis Andres was completely off guard revealing his vulnerability, the engrossed delirium of his love.

"It was as I suspected. You are taken by another woman," exclaimed Don Santos. Luis Andres was so startled that he dropped the sketchbook. The breeze revealed the various pages dedicated to the woman. He quickly moved to pick up his valuable possession but not before Don Santos, who was quicker despite his age. He recognized the girl to be Clarissa. It was the hired help's daughter. He was not amused. However it explained why he might have left so abruptly. "What is this?" As Don Santos looked at him angrily, Luis Andres said nothing. He just stared at his hand that held his most treasured item.

"I want you to explain her!" Don Santos stated sarcastically. Luis Andres moved forward extending his hand to retrieve the sketches from him. Don Santos looked at him severely and gave him the sketchbook. Luis Andres had never been so bold with his father. "I see you prefer to be silent about the matter. Well maybe those things are best kept secret. I will warn you now to maintain discretion about your affair with this woman. I will not have you in any way embarrass the family." Don Santos' demeanor was intimidating and harsh as he spoke. He stared hard at his son. He would not leave his chamber until Luis Andres understood his obligation to the family. Luis Andres felt the flames of rage gradually brewing within him. He felt suffocated by his father's reprimands. He wanted to lash out at him. This was not what he wanted for himself. Don Santos could see the range of thoughts that faceted Luis Andres' eyes.

"Luis Andres, it would not touch my heart to withdraw all your luxuries and strip you from my testament, despite you being my only son. A penniless existence has no worth; you could not survive my boy." Luis Andres turned away from him, clutching his fist as to control his temper. Don Santos continued aggressively. "I do not care how many mistresses you decide to have but they must be invisible and kept away from the image of the family. Do you understand?"

Luis Andres looked into the darkness of the evening. The truth of the matter is that he wanted to make things right and drop the facade that he had weaved for himself. It was too late. He would have to follow through the path he had initially started. The wedding would proceed as planned. "I will do as you have planned and marry Aimee," replied Luis Andres civilly.

"And the girl?" inquired Don Santos.

"The girl will be my quiet affair," he added coldly.

"Good." Don Santos walked out shutting the door behind him.

Luis Andres went to the window and clutched his sketchbook hard. A single teardrop streamed down leaving emptiness in him.

30

The day of Luis Andres' wedding with Aimee was fast approaching. Jean-Claude was traveling to see Clarissa. He found himself in the most vicarious position. The golden dream nestled in the high hills was coming to view. Clarissa stood outside enjoying nature's company.

She had become with child; bearing the seed of man's immortality. Clarissa beamed with the splendor of motherhood. The vision of radiance stole his breath away. Clarissa could not have imagined how her innocent beauty eclipsed the wild flowers she held in her hands. The news of Clarissa's expectancy would be tumultuous joy to his friend's sad disposition.

The gleam of delight sprung from the recesses of her eyes at the sight of Jean-Claude. Clarissa's separation from Luis Andres had been a torrent of solitude. It was the memories of the splendor of their love that engraved in her heart provided her with the strength to succumb her fears. She had matured so quickly in their time apart. The arrival of her child was a vessel of life whose budding rose had ripened exquisitely. Jean-Claude moved toward her with a package in his hand. Clarissa waited anxiously to hear about Luis Andres and his return home.

"Clarissa, what a surprise. You are expecting and looking lovely at that."
She was embarrassed by his compliment and looked down briefly. "Luis
Andres will be happy to know that he has a son on the way."

The words served to bring an inner brightness that exuberated from her
face, "I miss him greatly. I want to tell him how he has given me such
happiness with this child in me." She spoke with such devotion and
conviction that Jean-Claude was envious for a moment of his friend's
fortune.

He had come to see that life was a journey made of blessings that
accompanied most often by struggles. The obstacles were none other
than our inhibition and fears. The chances of happiness were simple and
attainable. It could not be corrupted nor shrouded by deception or it
would spoil. Luis Andres was a fool. He had happiness at hand and he
was aware of it. He was risking everything for nothing other than shallow
ends that would have little bearings but tragedy.

"Luis Andres sent this for you. He wanted me to tell you that his life has
little meaning without you. His family has made it difficult for him. He
needs to stay longer until he can resolve the situation."

Tears clouded Clarissa as she attempted to wipe them with the hand that
was holding her flowers. Jean-Claude took a handkerchief from his coat
to hand to her. He did not want to be affected by her and yet he was.
Clarissa was transparent with her feelings. She held her heart in her hand
so openly for everyone to see. This made her susceptible to being
seriously hurt. Yet despite this vulnerability, she was free. There was
something liberating about not being occupied with guarding one's true
nature and appearance. "I apologize for being so inconsiderate. Please
come in and I will prepare a meal and coffee." She took the package from
him and walked into the house.

The azure of the dark twilight was the canopy that they sat under while
sipping coffee. The meal she had prepared was wonderfully palatable.
Clarissa had placed the package on the table and placed the flowers in a
thin vase to give the room atmosphere. He understood now the place of
heaven Luis Andres had left behind and the anguish he faced daily
without her. They contemplated the blue night. "Will you tell Luis

Andres he must try to come home soon before his child is born? I can wait but hopefully he will resolve the problem with his family." She thought out loud as she spoke to him. "He is everything to me Jean-Claude. I am sad that I cannot be with him. I do hope that maybe our baby could bring the family together," she smiles melancholically.

Jean-Claude nodded his head in agreement although it unlikely. He was not accustomed to speaking with a woman in such a way. Her words were fluid and moved through the soul. Jean-Claude was burdened by the oath to his friend. However, Clarissa would be destroyed if she ever discovered Luis Andres' marriage to Aimee. It was his obligation to stop the treachery from continuing and to make things right. The deception would destroy them somehow. "Clarissa I will bring back Luis Andres. He will be here to see his child born. Do not worry; all will resolve itself." He succeeded in making her smile.

She took another sip of her coffee and looked to the sky imagining him in the moonlight. "At least we share the moonlight and the stars above us. It is comforting to know that he may be looking at the same moon and stars and thinking of me." She blew the moon a kiss. "I love you darling Luis Andres." Jean-Claude said nothing and let her enjoy her reverie. He was enamored by the immense love she had for his friend.

It was beguiling for Jean-Claude the depth of influence this trip had on his person. The boundaries of senses appeared to stretch and enrich his perspective on his view of life. He felt beckoned to try and change the course of things in his friend's life. He had committed himself to saving Luis Andres from the ultimate mistake of marrying Aimee. Clarissa was the lamb that stood to be sacrificed. He was taken by the simplicity that she represented. He could not be sure if Luis Andres had the strength to oppose the social norms placed by his class. He realized more clearly the injustices that his class imposed on those less fortunate. It was not enough that they were marginalized and mistreated for being born into poverty yet their spirit soared in the most elusive manner. They appreciated any happiness bestowed on them and held unto it with their life.

Jean-Claude walked into the house looking for Luis Andres only to discover that he had accompanied his father on an expedition of some sort. The day of the wedding was at hand as the preparations flourished around the hacienda. Many of the guests had arrived for the anticipated event. Doña Santos and Aimee were occupied with all the arrangements. Alexis was seated outside enjoying the warmth of the day as Jean-Claude approached him. "Alexis, have you seen Luis Andres?"

Alexis stared at him curiously. "Where have you been? I was beginning to think you went back to your country." He remarked cynically.

Jean-Claude was not in the mood, "Have you seen him!"

Alexis retorted abruptly, "He went with his father. I don't know if we will see him tonight, with the wedding and the entire guests arriving. I understood that they would be staying close to the church or something."

Jean-Claude grew increasingly anxious, "What do you mean he is not staying here tonight? The wedding is tomorrow."

Alexis was intrigued with Jean-Claude's behavior. "Of course the wedding is tomorrow. It is customary for the bride not to be seen by the groom. I imagine that is why he is staying away from the hacienda."

Jean-Claude's frustration became obvious, "Damn him!"

Alexis was taken aback by his exclamation. "I am sure you can see him tomorrow in church before the ceremony. Whatever it is you have to tell him I am sure it can wait," he said amusingly.

Jean-Claude gave him a vexed expression and walked away.

Luis Andres stood in the quiet sanctuary of the church. The candles illuminated the ceiling with iridescent flex of the cathedral. He stood holding his rosary attentively. Jean-Claude walked into the church observing his dear friend. "Luis Andres, I have come back from seeing Clarissa. She waits for you."

140

Luis Andres put the rosary in his pocket. He was reminded of the time he overheard her confession about her feelings for him. The many times they had met in church to discuss their affection and future together. It was disappointing to feel that he had failed her. He would now be committed to Aimee against his will. He wrestled with dropping everything and seeking her out.

"Is she well? I cannot go to her yet Jean-Claude even though I desperately want to." He pauses for a moment. "Don't you understand I cannot?"

Jean-Claude felt his temper rise to his head. He was jolted by the fury that grew so volcanic. It erupted and he slapped him. "You coward! Are you not tired of all this hypocrisy? Be a man and make a choice. Who will it be Clarissa or Aimee? Remember I know whom you love. You owe it to yourself to make Clarissa happy. It is not fair to continue with this masquerade."

Luis Andres' eyes burned with reciprocated anger as he stared at his closest friend. His ego had been injured and he reacted accordingly with much emotion. He could not believe that he had raised his hand against him. He felt a razor sharpness striking him. "I see you have turned against me Jean-Claude. I would have never expected that from you ... anyone but you."

Jean-Claude was trembling and feeling that he was pinning his friend to see the truth of his decision. "I am tired of the lie Luis Andres. We must put a stop to it. You cannot marry Aimee when you care for Clarissa. She is now your family. You have a responsibility to her."

Luis Andres looked angrily. "I know I do but I have a responsibility to fulfill as the only heir to this family. I never expected this to get so complicated. Anyway, Clarissa has a better life than she could have had with anyone. We will conform."

Jean-Claude could see that he would not move. "You are the greatest fool if you think that it's that simple. When Clarissa discovers the deception she will loathe you. It is presumptuous of you to think that she is better off living this lie. No my friend ... if anything she was better off with her family and that boy who loved her. She left everything for you."

The words burned through Luis Andres' flesh, to the interior of his soul. It was unbearable yet he stood steadfast to his stubbornness. "I don't want to hear anymore! I will proceed with this marriage. It is done." He stormed out of the church.

Jean-Claude felt the chill breeze sweep by as he quietly whispered to himself, "She is having your child, my friend."

31

The sight of being back home was mixed with feelings of regret and nostalgia. The excursion to locate Clarissa had ended in nothing. He had become orphaned again to everything he loved. Roberto was exhausted and his spirit had persevered despite all the anguish he had experienced. He wandered into town only to discover the procession of a wedding.

The curiosity was great that he followed them toward the church. He stood outside the steps waiting to see who it might be. It became apparent by the conversation of the locals that it was the anticipated wedding of Luis Andres and La Niña Aimee. Roberto was consumed with rage at the news. The zealous anger and hatred for Luis Andres blinded him. He was determined to find Luis Andres and unleash everything that was festering beneath his bowels. He headed to the hacienda in hopes of reaching Luis Andres before the ceremony. He arrived at the door only to find Jean-Claude outside.

They both stared each other before Roberto muttered, "Where is that bastard Luis Andres?"

Jena-Claude was startled by his sudden appearance and walked over to him. He was steaming with madness and showed disdain for their social class. "I am sorry but everyone is at the Church. As a matter of fact I was heading there myself."

He was trying to be civil to a determined Roberto. It was apparent that his demeanor had altered since he last saw him. There behind those masqueraded eyes of anger hid deep sadness.

"How could he be so selfish ... to have the audacity to marry someone else when he has Clarissa?" He spoke to him with so much heated anger. "I knew he would abandon her and soon forget her when I love her so. Curse your class for everything! Now what has become of Clarissa?"

Jean-Claude was defensive despite knowing his conscious wore heavily at the sight of this destroyed man. He wanted to console him but feared angering him further. "I am sorry for you. I agree that my friend is undeserving of her but he does love her."

Roberto glared at the insinuation. He could not compose himself and angrily raised his voice. "If he loved her, would he have deceived her in the manner that he did? Would he have separated her from those who loved her? Of course not! His self absorbed behavior has cost Clarissa integrity and her parents!"

Jean-Claude was startled by his remarks. "What do you mean that her parents are lost to her?"

Roberto did not expect such concern from his voice. His anger subsided slightly and revealed the sorrow behind the loss of her parents. "Her parents perished in a tragic death while in search of her. So you see your friend's irresponsible actions have cost Clarissa the love of her only family."

Jean-Claude was lost for words. This news would break Clarissa's heart. Could she recover from such an unexpected recovery? He wondered while Roberto continued. "Soon after burying them, away from their land, I sought to find Clarissa in Mexico City. This is where we heard they were headed. After months of searching with no success, I returned home tired only to find he is getting married to another woman."

Jean-Claude felt atrocious as the guilt of his participation in the deceit was latching to his heart, squeezing any possible justification of their actions. His thoughts were engulfed in restituting the damage done. Luis Andres had made the painful decision to marry Aimee. Therefore it was only just for Clarissa to move on with her life with Roberto. He loved her despite everything. Luis Andres would probably resent him forever and likely never forgive him for aiding Roberto with Clarissa.

"Roberto if you would like I could take you to her. I know where she is." Jean-Claude said softly, "You must promise to care for her especially during this time."

Roberto was in disbelief. This man had extended himself to take him to her. He felt a ray of hope rise from the black hole that he was living. "Yes I would be indebted to you. I need to see Clarissa," with desperation in his voice.

Jean-Claude felt convicted and suggested that he take her away. "It is best you both start anew away from all the sadness. Please take her away. She is a very special individual. The purest creature I have ever met."

It was unsettling to Roberto the amount of concern that Jean-Claude revealed for Clarissa. It almost appeared that he had deeper feelings than he wanted exposed. He felt it best not to disclose his observation but merely followed him to Clarissa.

32

The evening's warm wind danced with her white dress as she stood outside pondering on the sun setting. Her mind was preoccupied with a rising uneasiness that something was wrong. It was a fear that was determined to breach the delicate layer of her happiness. She attributed her condition to the long absence of her beloved Luis Andres. The sound of horses approaching made her heart dive with anticipation. It seemed like long ago since she last set eyes on her Luis Andres. She was reminiscent of their days together and now he had come back. She would run to him and divulge the news of her pregnancy. The silhouette of two men came walking gradually toward her. It soon became clear that the image of the men before her was not Luis Andres.

The sight of Roberto suffocated Clarissa breath. She was motionless as he treaded toward her. She was overpowered with streams of emotions. The past came showering quickly as his eyes came to view and the release of tears found themselves flowing down her face. The longing to see her after so much tribulation had finally arrived. Clarissa stood in the bloom of life. She was radiant with her white dress moving to the gentle current. He was startled and the flames of jealousy soared at the disappointment of her obvious expectant condition. He comprehended Jean-Claude's apprehension of disclosing any further information about her. Clarissa was carrying Luis Andres' child. Yet as he walked to her and witnessed the tears run down her cheeks, it extinguished the fire within. It did not matter for he still loved her regardless of the child she was having. It was part of her and that is all that mattered. Clarissa and the child were innocent in the deception concocted by Luis Andres. The struggle that remained was to tell her the inopportune news of her parents and the man whom she loved exceedingly.

"Oh Roberto," catching her breath.

Jean-Claude stood behind him, witnessing their interaction. His heart was grave about his involvement in such treachery. He waited patiently for the proper opportunity to ask for forgiveness for the ordeal.

Roberto smiled and sweetly spoke to her. "Clarissa my eyes have waited to see you again. It has been far too long since our last meeting, I missed you heartedly."

Clarissa found it difficult to express all that was also bottled in her heart. Her Roberto displayed a broad compassion in his eyes even with the sorrow that remained. He had aged slightly from the previous time she had seen him. It could not be denied that her abrupt departure contributed to the change of his countenance. She wondered how her family was fairing. The key was that Roberto would be able to tell her everything about her parents. She nervously spoke to him.

"The news of my sudden wedding must have been a surprise. It was like a dream that was missing you and my parents."

Roberto gave a quick look to Jean-Claude. He looked down while listening attentively. Clarissa felt the uneasiness come over them.

"Please Roberto forgive me for the manner in which I told you. I was afraid of seeing you and that you would not understand how I felt. It is just that I love him so much. I could not stand hurting you when you have been so honest with your feelings for me." He continued to look at the ground trying to conceal his sorrow as she spoke. "I thought how easy it would be just to love you but my heart was inclined to follow him and made the choice for me. Please do not be angry any longer. I am completely happy."

Roberto moved toward Clarissa with open arms. It was hurtful to hear such honesty from her. He thought of how she would react after knowing the real truth. He embraced her like a child he wanted to protect against any harm. "I do not know how to tell you." She could feel his heart pacing quickly beneath his shirt. There was urgency desperately trying to come out.

"Please tell me whatever it may be." She was unaware of the apocalyptic nature of the revelation.

Roberto's voice was low, damped with a tragic tone. "Clarissa" with a pause before uttering the difficult words, "Your parents are dead."

A flash of images moved before her eyes. The dreams that haunted her were foreshadowing what had come to pass. A cold shudder moved through her spine as a cloud of darkness veiled her and the tremulous sobs came, rising from her soul. She clung to Roberto in disbelief. "No, it cannot be. They cannot be dead. Please Roberto!"

He held her gently in his arms. "Clarissa you must be stronger still yet ... Luis Andres never married you. He has married someone else."

33

Clarissa pushed him away as the tears roamed freely. "Why? Why must you be so cruel and tell such lies. He has married me!" She looked to Jean-Claude who watched the tragedy unfurl before him. Clarissa moved toward Jean-Claude for affirmation. "Tell him that it is not so. You were at our wedding. Tell him please." Her voice pleaded with him to decipher the truth. He looked at her with shame. The truth manifested itself with the look in his eyes. Clarissa knew that she had been deceived.

Roberto moved to help her in her anguish but she pushed him away, dismissing his hands. She looked at them both broken hearted. Clarissa ran off into the wilderness.

Jean-Claude held Roberto's arm to keep him from following her. "She needs time alone Roberto. It has been so much for her to support." He followed her with his eyes until she no longer was.

Clarissa moved through the dark earth seeking to find solace from her desperation. The internal injury to her spirit was mortal and gradually consuming her. The sweeping sadness resonated in her thoughts at the cold awareness that Luis Andres had married someone else. The silent eyes of Jean-Claude confirmed the treachery. She stopped grasping her arms, holding herself trying to find some warmth in the chill that enveloped her. Her heart sank in despair. She grasped for air as the emotions brewed and erupted into cries of anguish. Her words hardly audible came dipped into salted drops that preserved the tormented truth. "I was nothing to you just another moment's pleasure, a fleeting memory. I am now reduced to drink the bitter juice that finds little comfort now. I am alone; yielding to this drowning emptiness that I must swallow." Her cries continued as she looked around the green earth about her. "The bitter prophesy foretold by those around me. How sweet was the fruit of your deceit Luis Andres? You have killed my dream and buried my family and me."

Her body folded as her knees crashed to the ground. A pang struck her stomach, "Oh Virgin of Mother, what is to become of this child and me?" Clarissa's white dress soon took on a tainted crimson color that started below her abdominal. A wave of blows attacked her belly, crippling her further. The dress was drenched with the tint of her blood. The sight of this made her release an abhorrent cry within her already weak disposition. The darkness descended, veiling her eyes as she embraced the ground.

The agonizing wail could be heard echoing through the air. Roberto and Jean-Claude knew instantly that it was Clarissa. They ran to her, dreading the worst. The bleak discovery was heartbreaking. It was an image that would haunt them forever. She lay on the ground vulnerable and bathing in a pool of her own blood that had seeped through her white dress. She was like a wounded animal waiting for death among the natural darkness of the grass.

Roberto and Jean-Claude stood for a second transfixed by the wretched image. It had a profound impression on their spirit. Roberto was engulfed in fear, chastising himself for the poisonous words that had Clarissa on the verge of mortality. He carefully lifted her body from the earth that welcomed her. The shadow of death followed as the trace of her blood paved the way.

"Clarissa, do not leave me. I cannot survive your loss as well. I will find myself alone again." He sobbed and held her close to his body as they walked to the house. "Please make an effort, at least live for your unborn child."

150

Her eyes fluttered giving some remnants of hope. They placed her frail body on the bed. Jean-Claude sought a blanket from the closet. He helped place it over her. He ran to fetch a doctor from the near town below while Roberto stood steadfast by her side. He lit a candle to remove the ever present night. The flower of bloom had lost its luster, swept away were the petals. Roberto prayed for forgiveness. He had allowed jealousy to consume his spirit not considering the repercussion of his abrupt words. The soft moan of pain could be heard from her lips.

"Roberto, Roberto, don't cry."

She moved her hand slowly to get to his. The pain in her body continued as she spoke to him in whispers. He stood up to try to get something to ease her anguish. She seized his hand, "Please stay with me. The pain will soon pass." A gloss struggled to take hold over her eyes. "The grief I now feel is a reminder of my weakness. I do not know why our lives turn out in a certain ways. I was attracted to the sun and flew close. My ashes will be scattered here on this earth."

Roberto could not fathom the way she was talking, so ready to embrace death. The affliction he was experiencing was another nightmare.

"Roberto, forgive me for the grief I have caused you. I promise that in heaven I will look out for you and shower my blessings."

Roberto looked at her, upset by the manner she was speaking. "Why do you welcome death so quickly? He is not worth your life, Clarissa! And what of the child?"

She was moved by the immense love he had for her. "Roberto, do not cry for me. I wish I had the wisdom that I have now. Maybe my decision would have been different. My misfortune is that I love him despite everything. My tragedy is that I must live without him in this world. Roberto death lies next to me speaking sweet sounds and holds my beautiful child. I have to depart this earth with him so that I may carry my child to heaven."

Roberto nods his head in disagreement with tears blinding him. "You are wrong Clarissa. A new life is before you, the opportunity to have a different type of happiness."

Clarissa wept, "Roberto it has been decided."

34

Luis Andres had completed the task of marrying Aimee De La Madrid. He had fulfilled his obligation to the family making them happy. He buried the desolate void in his heart as he lay next to his newly acquired bride. The consummation of their union was just an intoxicated pleasure marred by the secrecy of his haunting love for Clarissa. He lulled himself to dream of her. Luis Andres saw Clarissa before him in this vision, gazing at him. She was draped in white with flowers in her hair. He was struck by how angelic and transparent she appeared. There in her look lay a depth of revelation that carried with it a deep sadness despite the smile.

He was overcome with shame and regret. It was now clear that he had made a fallible mistake in his decision to marry someone else. The paradise of his dream was Clarissa; yet he reviled it through his desire to have it both ways. Clarissa's fate was sealed by his deception.

The palette of colors in this reverie was showered in melancholic splendor. He found it easy to unravel the dark confession of his deception. Her expression was ever compassionate in light of the awful truth. Her aura revealed an awareness of his transgression as she wore a veil of sadness on her lovely face. "I am dreaming, dreaming of the sweet heaven that stands before me ... forgive me. What courage do I have to stand before you and ask for forgiveness? I am undeserving of you now.

My intentions were distorted by my own selfish desires. I never intended to hurt you Clarissa. You are the person I adore most in this world. My reasoning does not justify the choices I have made on our part. I understand the heavy price of my decision. I have sacrificed your happiness and have painted your eyes blue with disillusionment. I have offended you profoundly and such is my shame."

Luis Andres yearned to touch her warmth. She walked slowly toward him like in dreams and her movement entranced him. He moved forward; fearful that she was just a mirage ready to disappear. He embraced her tightly and felt a comfort in his soul as he caressed her hair. He wanted to stay with her like that forever. Luis Andres found himself weeping as Clarissa moved closer to whisper something in his ear that moved him. "I love you, Luis Andres." A feeling took hold of him as she withdrew back from him. He longed to kiss those lips as her head drew away, falling back toward the ground. His arms moved to catch her from the fall as he called her name.

"Clarissa!"

He woke from the lurid dream in a sweat of anxiousness. In a disheveled state he looked for his rosary with frenzy, which he had placed in a drawer away from sight. He took it; held it tight and brought it to his lips. He kissed it ever so tenderly unaware that Aimee was watching him.

"Luis Andres, what are you doing?" exclaimed Aimee.

Luis Andres startled by her voice gripped the rosary hard and the beads broke into pieces. They fell to the ground scattered all over the floor. He could not remove the bad premonition that something was not well with Clarissa. He felt a dark dread that quickly covered his piece of gilded civility. "Please I would prefer you not to help!"

She stood quietly, observing him in silent humiliation. It was clear that her relationship with Luis Andres had been defined. It would be a relationship based on appearances only.

154

35

As the dusk of day approached, Roberto was close to Clarissa trying to maintain his sanity despite the misfortune that was in front of him. The frailty of Clarissa was becoming more evident with the passing of time. He wondered what was taking Jean-Claude so long to come with the physician. It was difficult to conjure up the hope to believe that she would be well. The shadow of death now clouded her face.

Clarissa spoke reflectively to him, "Roberto I want you to promise me something. I want you not to lose your heart. You have gone through so much heartache and it is not always fair. I know not what these obstacles have done to you but you must swear that it will not change the kind-hearted Roberto I love. Please do not bear Luis Andres any ill will. His regrets will soon follow. I have forgiven him as you have forgiven me for all the pain I have caused you."

Roberto was annoyed. It stung his heart to see how considerate she was of the man who had been the cause of so much grief. He could not deny her anything even though his heart was bitter with sorrow. He nodded his head reluctantly as he compromised and agreed. "I ... promise."

She smiled as she held her pain. She grabbed his hand and felt a dizziness taking over. Her vision was becoming blurred with confusion. Roberto saw Jean-Claude rush into the room with what appeared to be a physician. Clarissa could hardly make them out. The shadow of colors seemed to swirl before her as she heard the resounding anguish of Roberto.

"Clarissa, please hold on."

Jean-Claude distraught held back his tears. She found herself traveling into a tunnel of darkness that drove her at a fast pace. A glimpse of light waited ahead as she voiced with all her might the name of Luis Andres.

36

Clarissa woke abruptly to the sound of the church bells. It had been only a dream as she looked at the necklace around her neck. The emotions were all too real. It was puzzling to have assimilated the pain of the other Clarissa of so long ago. She walked to the window and looked at the moonlight. A sweet breeze came by to kiss her as she wept at the loss of her heart.

Meanwhile Luis Andres in his old age went to his bureau and locked himself in his studies. He opened the drawer and took out his treasure box that contained the sketches of his great love. He contemplated the memory of her face and the sad reminder of her. It was the vigil of her memory that he carried in his heart and soul. It was agonizing to remember the grief that he had suffered at the discovery of Clarissa's untimely death and that of their unborn child. It was the unhappy hour that tainted his soul with regret when he hurried to see her; only to find that she was deceased.

He would never forget when he walked into the room that mourned, as she laid on their bed in an eternal slumber. How he ran to her side, a broken man, oblivious to the presence of Roberto and Jean-Claude who quietly shed tears. The same home that offered him heaven now left him alone to deal with the emptiness of his heart. Clarissa was beautiful in her sleep that adorned her with fresh flowers; a teardrop still remained holding back until his arrival. It was mysteriously sad as he removed the tear from her face. Luis Andres fell apart in his sea of grief as he held her cold body in his arms. He kissed those lips seeking hope and unearthing the truth that she was lost forever.

The tears fell unto the sketches of Clarissa that he had painted many years earlier. He caressed the pictures remembering the sweetness of her lips that he had tasted earlier in the church. It was the lips of this new Clarissa that he had encountered in the church that somehow held the memory of his old Clarissa. His penitence had come to an end and he would soon be reunited with her forever. Luis Andres took the rosary that had become part of his entire life. He muttered her name with his tired breath ...

"Clarissa..."

A strange wind unexpectedly opened the doors of his bureau that led to his garden. The wind was a familiar sweet light voice coming to find him. It was the sweet breeze that stole his soul away. His hand dropped and the rosary with the sketches flew around his body finally resting on the floor. The church bells could be heard simultaneously and the quietness of the blue night was all that remained.

37

The late hour brought the gloom news of the discovery that Don Andres
had passed away. Luis Alberto and Father Roberto had trouble opening
the doors to his studies. They broke into his bureau after much effort of
calling his name and finally budging the door. Luis Alberto was Don
Andres' only son from his marriage with Aimee de la Madrid. He rushed
to his father peacefully at rest in his chair. The sight of his stiffness
caused Luis Alberto to fall to his knees. He moved to hold his father's
lifeless body in the hope that he was merely in a deep sleep. He sought to
feel the light breath of his slumber and found only silence. Luis Alberto
hugged his father tightly acknowledging the terrible realization that he is
no more. He wept for his father; the devoted man that Don Andres was.
He was very generous with his love to him, despite the traces of sadness
in his countenance.

Luis Alberto loved and respected his father and understood that he
carried a burden of secrecy that he would not talk about. Maybe now he
could relinquish all his sorrow by the chains of his past. Father Roberto
stared at the man he once hated and ultimately learned to forgive. He
noticed the rosary on the floor, next to the scattered sketches of her.
Father Roberto picked them up and drew a deep breath looking out to the
open doors that led to the garden. "Indeed how strange that all the
suffering and sadness are now gone. Only fragments of recollections
linger."

Luis Alberto moved to look at Father Roberto who spoke somberly in his contemplation. The sketches of Clarissa fell from his hands and landed close to him. He stared at them intensely behind those watered eyes. In a broken voice he asked who the girl was.

Father Roberto glanced at the drawing with nostalgic pain; "She is a voice from your father's past that has now found peace."

Luis Alberto took the sketch from the ground and said nothing.

38

The light showers scattered about as Clarissa stood alone by the grave of Don Andres. She let the tears roll down her cheeks as she measured her loss. The dirt was moist in her hand as she handled it gently. She was reminiscent of all the events that had transpired from the moment she arrived to this very minute, in this enchanted place known as Guanajuato. She was widowed by the sudden departure of the man she learned to love in her dream. How could she reconcile her feelings that moved within her? The image of his face scarred her memory. It was cruel fate to be left alone. The illusions would remain to cloud her heart in this joyous sorrow of living a dream.

She wept inconsolably.

The sweet breeze brought an unexpected voice behind that somber figure. He lightly tapped her on the shoulder. "Why do you cry over my father's grave?"

Clarissa stood silent for a moment before turning her head. "I felt like I knew him somehow."

She was startled by the man's striking resemblance to Luis Andres. He was young and handsome with the slight difference in the color of his eyes that were green like the meadow. His afflicted pain was somehow intercepted with a new possibility as he looked at her with penetrating interest.

He was taken aback by the girl that was exactly like the sketch he held in his pocket. The girl of many years ago who had bewitched his father Luis Andres ... and now enraptured him. He took the sketch out from his pocket and handed it to her as the rain fell on them.

She looked at the sketch and held it to her bosom as she wept. Luis Alberto felt the need to erase the sorrow that covered her lovely face. He took his jacket and placed it on her shoulders to cover her from the rain.

His voice reached to her cooing heart. "I hope I can fill the absence left by your pain. I believe we were intended to meet, Clarissa. I am Luis Alberto at your service." He held his hand to her.

Speechless, she smiled and took his hand. The wind hailed as it disentangled the dark clouds, clearing the path for the horizon of a new start. The song of nature was now sweet as they walked together, away from the distant sorrow that now lay to rest.

######

About the author:

Jacqueline Fernandez was born in Southern California and graduated with a degree in Social Sciences. Her love for literature, music and history has played a major role in her creative process as a writer. It is her belief that in light of the challenges and imperfections we face as a human race we are still resilient. There is a beauty in all the diverse cultures that make up the world despite the ugliness that can exist in our spirit. It is the palate of all the assorted ethnicities that create the canvas of life which she respects and love. There is color, music, and poetry in the way people live. All individuals are a ballad that moves with different rhythms and define our humanity, mirroring an array of complex emotions that range from sorrow, vanity, fear, and happiness. She is influenced and moved by society's constant struggle to understand itself. Her vision is the desire to go beyond tolerance and move toward compassion and kindness and enjoy our multicultural differences. To know that we are distinct individuals yet not autonomous from the world we live in.

Connect with the author online:

WORKSBYJFERNANDEZ – Facebook Page

Visit Jacqueline's website for up-to-date news
and her other available titles.

www.worksbyjfernandez.com